I0634861

Rhoda Broughton

Joan - A Tale

Vol. II

Rhoda Broughton

Joan - A Tale
Vol. II

ISBN/EAN: 9783337079109

Printed in Europe, USA, Canada, Australia, Japan

Cover: Foto ©Andreas Hilbeck / pixelio.de

More available books at **www.hansebooks.com**

JOAN

A Tale

BY

RHODA BROUGHTON

AUTHOR OF

"COMETH UP AS A FLOWER" "RED AS A ROSE IS SHE" "GOOD-BYE SWEET-
HEART!" "NANCY" "NOT WISELY BUT TOO WELL."

IN THREE VOLUMES
VOL. II.

LONDON
RICHARD BENTLEY AND SON
Publishers in Ordinary to Her Majesty the Queen
1876

(All Rights Reserved)

JOAN.

PART I.—*Continued.*

CHAPTER XVI.

SINCE that dread Sunday, two whole months and one half one have now rolled by. August is come : the month on which our short and chilly summer generally tries to concentrate all its heat.

This year, at all events, the sun seems to have saved all his ardour till now, and to be pouring forth his gathered fierceness on the throbbing heads of man and beast; on the pining flowers and the dull trees that have lost all the jocund freshness of their June prime. There has been no rain for a fortnight, and every day—every day an untiring sickly stare of sunshine. Joan's little attic-room, with its low ceiling seeming to press down on her panting face, with its small and blindless window, is nothing short of an oven. Unspeakably she dreads the night, which will consign her to it—the sleepless night, when, gaspingly, with strained eyes, she looks for the dawn—the dawn that no bird-voices now usher in. It is only the comfortable sound of the far cold plunging sea that seems to keep her alive. How far rather would she lie all night on the burnt grass at the sun-dial foot, watched by the cool kind stars.

"No one who lives in a large house has any idea of what heat is!" she says to herself, sitting nerveless and pallid by the drawing-room window, through which, at the passing of every harvest-wain or more briskly rolling carriage, a great choking

volley of white dust pours over the hedge
and into the room. For a wonder, she has
the apartment to herself; and, also for a
wonder, she is idle. Joan is not often idle.
Witness the frequent darns in the carpet;
the new antimacassars; the girls' new bonnets;
Mrs. Moberley's new evening cap (less abun-
dantly flowered, of a soberer style of archi-
tecture than any of its predecessors); Diana's
thumbed lesson-books. For the moment she
is absolutely unemployed. Her eyes stray
with a wistful languor out of window to the
dancing gnats and the sere hot herbage, and
her figure, which her black gown fits less
accurately than it did, leans dejectedly back
in her chair.

It is impossible to grow fat upon air; and
during this hot weather her palate absolutely
refuses the coarse food that is offered to it.
Two months and a half, and in all that time
not one bright spot! And yet she has seen
Wolferstan! How many times? She is too
hot to count, but is mistily aware that if she

added together the number of their meetings they would amount to a considerable sum. Not one bright spot! She mentally corrects herself. Yes, one!—two, even. Once, when suddenly he came upon her, by the wash of the morning waves; and yet once again, when they sat side by side in the wood's green twilight, and looked down the foxglove's speckled throat. But his visits here! Hot as she is, a still hotter flush steals over her body at the recollection.

She sits up and gasps. Which was worst, the day on which Bell asked him for his photograph, forcing her own upon him; or the day on which Sarah emptied all over him the tepid, lumpy, melted butter at luncheon? For her precautions have been vain. He has lunched here; has seen the tablecloth, with its veteran stains; the foggy spoons; the jagged cutlery; has had a cracked plate violently thrust upon him by Sarah's raven-black finger and thumb; and been hospitably over-loaded with underdone mutton, which he was equally unable to swallow or hide. His flowers too! the divine flowers in their delicate plenty that he so often sent her, until one day, with miserable scarlet cheeks and lowered eyes, with halting tongue and broken voice, she begged him to desist.

Flowers are messengers from heaven, but even they may be too dearly bought. They are too dearly paid for at the price of Bell's envious raillery, Mrs. Moberley's jovially hopeful prognostics, and Micky's angry persiflage.

Looking back on the past twelve weeks, what has she left her, but an impression of mortification, onions, and purgatorial heat?

Pshaw! this weather is asphyxiating! She whisks about her pocket-handkerchief in the effort to make a little air-current, but in vain. This is in the morning, and you may imagine that in the afternoon it is not likely to be much cooler. Yet the afternoon sees Joan trudging along the Helmsley road. What was her idle, passive, shielded morning

heat compared to her active sun-struck afternoon heat ?

Mrs. Moberley is spending the day with a
friend; Bell is in bed with a sick headache ;
it seems ill-natured to allow Diana to go
alone ; and to Helmsley some one must go,
to remonstrate with the baker on leaving the
establishment breadless.

Oh, why could not he have chosen a cooler
day on which to forget their dole of loaves ?

In spiritless silence, with throbbing heads
and powdery feet and faint limbs, the two
girls take their way along the gridiron of the
high-road ; their very brains feeling as if they
were frying, bubbling, steaming in their
heads. They have reached the town ; have
trodden the hot pavement, have done their
errand, have again left the burning flags, and
are on their way back again. Di has not
even had spirit to peep at the new percales
in the draper's window, or give one passing
glance to the awkward squad drilling and
grilling in the barrack-yard.

Now at least their faces are turned homewards. More than half of their ordeal is over. They are about midway between Helmsley and home, when their burnt and dazzled eyes catch sight of a carriage involved in dust, bowling briskly along to meet them : a well-turned out London carriage, smart servants, sleek lofty-mannered horses.

" It is Mrs. Wolferstan !" says Diana in an excited voice, a ray of life and animation streaming into her scorched fagged face ; " they have come down then at last ! I wonder will she bow to me ?"

The doubt is soon solved. As the barouche flashes past its sole inmate—a lady luxuriously stretched under a big sunshade, amid a sea of muslins—leans forward to bow and smile with accented civility.

" Is the world coming to an end ?" cries Diana, standing stock still in the dust, and gazing in astonishment after the retreating vehicle. " Mostly she looks as if she were not aware that there were such people on the earth's face! at this rate she will probably soon kiss us."

" Was that Colonel Wolferstan's mother?" asks Joan, surprised; having received only a transient impression of white veil, yellow hair, pink cheeks. " Why, she looked like a *young* lady!"

" I do not fancy that she looks very young when you take her to pieces," replies Diana sagely. " There's a good deal about her that does not belong to her! I wish," she adds regretfully, "that I was not so hot! I look so like Bell when I am red; I hope that she did not mistake me for her! do you think she did?"

" It is not in the least likely," replies Joan reassuringly, feeling meanwhile an inward conviction that to Mrs. Wolferstan's mind the Misses Moberley are a vague fact—a blur, endowed with no separate identity.

At length they have reached Portland Villa, and on entering the drawing-room find it no longer untenanted. Mrs. Moberley has returned. Bell has risen from her bed of sickness. Both are talking eagerly. The cause of the conversation is speedily discovered to be a small unopened note, which, held between Bell's finger and thumb, is having its superscription eagerly scanned.

On perceiving the two girls, she advances eagerly, holding it out to Joan, and crying:

"You have come at last! how you must have crawled! I could not have borne the suspense much longer; I should have been obliged to have opened it. Mrs. Wolferstan brought it," she goes on presently with voluble minuteness; "she came in her big barouche with the C. springs. She did not ask to come in; the footman left it!"

"Of course it is all that good fellow's doing," says Mrs. Moberley, with a familiarly fond allusion to Colonel Wolferstan; "he naturally likes his mother to be intimate with a family that he himself is on such very good terms with."

"And was Sarah," asks Joan faintly, her mind reverting to that fair being as she had last seen her, in torn apron, dirty cap stuck on awry, and with large smouches of black on her red cheeks—"was Sarah quite as she is now when Mrs. Wolferstan called? was her face quite as black?"

Bell nods ominously.

"Quite! Blacker!"

"I believe that she does it on purpose!" cries Diana in a rage.

"Probably," says Bell, her eyes greedily fastened on Joan, who has unfolded the billet, and, with tired white cheeks slightly pleasure-flushed, is reading it—"probably it is to invite us all to their school-feast."

"To luncheon more likely!" says Mrs. Moberley loftily; "naturally they wish to repay some of our hospitality."

"We must have a fly!" cries Bell sanguinely; "we never could walk in this weather—a two-horse fly!"

"I would not order it at once," says Diana

ironically. " I think you will find that our own equipages will be enough to convey us."

"Will you read it for yourselves?" asks Joan, coming to the end of the effusion, and holding it vaguely out to the company generally.

Bell eagerly snatches it and reads aloud :

" My dear Miss Dering,

"Will you overlook the informality of the request, and give us the pleasure of a visit? Your grandfather and I were such old friends that I cannot feel as if you were a stranger. If it suits you, will you come to us to-morrow for a week or ten days? I will send the carriage for you at any hour you like to name. Hoping that we shall be able to persuade you.

"Yours very truly,
"Sophia Wolferstan."

There is a blank silence.

"Was not it a mercy that we had not

ordered the fly?" asks Diana dryly, breaking it.

"We might not be in existence, for all the mention she makes of us!" says Bell in a wrathy voice; turning the note inside out to see whether the name of Moberley does not lurk in some overlooked postscript; "not even kind regards, or best remembrances."

"The obligation of our legs of mutton does not weigh so heavily as you thought, mother!" says Diana, who, never having been so sanguine as the others, is now less abashed than they, and can even see the humorous side of the situation.

"A week! ten days!" cries Bell, with an envious gasp, sinking down into a chair and letting her hands fall on her lap; "and the house will either be full of stylish London people, or you will have Anthony all to yourself! I declare I do not know which would be most delightful; what luck some people have!" She pursues a moment later, with a sound of tears in her voice: "And all through being highly connected. I declare it is enough to make one a Radical !"

" Stuff !" cries Mrs. Moberley crossly ; being hardly less disappointed than her daughter, and not averse from wreaking her ill-humour on her fellow sufferer. " Be thankful for the blessings you have, or as likely as not they will be taken away from you !"

" Thankful for the blessings we have !" echoes Bell, with peevish disrespect ; " that is nonsense, mother ! We have not any blessings to be thankful for, and you are not in the least thankful for them yourself."

" We have nothing but the cheese-parings and tallow candle-ends of life," says Diana resignedly, " but then we were meant for them ; Joan is not !"

CHAPTER XVII.

WERE Joan a wise woman she would, as she is well aware, reject Mrs. Wolferstan's overture. When Fate has seated you on a low rung of the social ladder, it is a mistake to allow yourself to be hoisted for a small and transient period on to a higher one. The temporary elevation only makes your low seat the more uneasy to you for ever after.

However little acclimatised she may think herself, yet there can be no doubt that three months' wear and tear have a little blunted the first sharp edge of astonished distaste.

That at the end of the ten days Sarah will
come upon her—Sarah, the smouched and
smutted—with the force of a new shock;
that Micky, Bell, the tablecloth, will all have
to be done over again. And Anthony! To
have him all to herself for ten days—as
Bell delicately puts it. And at the end of
the ten days, for there never yet were ten
days that did not end — how will she be
feeling ?

Ten days of unprotected exposure to the
joyful fondness of his faithless gray eyes, to
the sugared dishonesty of his smile, to the
easy, conscienceless, practised tenderness of
his words.

" I never used to be thought susceptible in
my good days—never !" she says to herself.
" I always laughed at them when they made
love to me. At the end of ten days shall I
be able to laugh ?"

Having thought for a moment and conscientiously answered " No !" she goes the
length of writing a note of refusal, which is

no sooner finished than it is torn into a hundred fragments.

"I am willing to pay for it," she cries out aloud—she is sitting in her own little room, her elbows resting on the table, her chin leant on her clasped hands — "however heavily I have to pay! No musk plant in a dry summer ever longed for rain as I do for a little happiness, a little enjoyment! I am dying of thirst. I must drink!" So, without giving herself time for reflection, she writes a line of acceptance and sends it off at once, lest she should again change her mind.

So it comes to pass that on the morrow, in the late afternoon, when the sun is beginning a little to relax the severity of his rule, she sets off. The big barouche stands at the door, the tall horses tossing their heads and digging unnecessary holes in the gravel with the hoofs of their supercilious forefeet, her aunt and cousins nodding farewell to her, with mixed envy and good-nature in their eyes.

Mrs. Moberley has indeed soon recovered

her good humour. "All work and no play makes Jack a dull boy!" she says jovially. "For my part, Joan, I am very glad that you should have a chance of shaking a loose leg now and then!"

"I will lend you my gutta-percha beads!" cries Diana. "At a little distance they look just like jet; and though they are rather apt to melt if one gets hot, yet that will not matter to you as you never do."

"Mind that you notice whether the dinner is carved off the table every day, or only when there is a party!" says Bell.

The last adieux are said; she has kissed all the dogs and told them that she is going to church, which, though not exactly true, conveys the right idea to their minds, viz., that it will be impious to attempt to follow her. Bell's parting adjuration to be sure not to forget to remember them to Colonel Wolferstan, screamed after her, dies away, drowned in the noise of the rolling wheels.

She is off! bowling swiftly along the well-
known bit of road, where she has so often
slowly trudged with weary feet, less weary
than her heart. With the thrifty idea of
making the most of it, she leans luxuriously
back on the cushions, and, lulled by the
smooth motion and the caress of the yielding
air, the idea strikes her, "Has it possibly
been a most ugly dream?" Is she driving
home to Dering to dinner? Will by-and-by
the four gray towers rise in familiar solemnity
on her sight against the lustre of the opulent
sky?

For one happy moment she nurses the idle
notion.   Then her eyes fall on the men-servants, and the dream dissolves ; the liveries
are different, and on the buttons the wolf
shows his snarling teeth where the Dering
lion was wont to ramp. Through the iron
gates, between whose bars Diana and she had
thrust their envious hot faces in meagre
survey on the day after her arrival; through
the park, where, above the deep green

bracken, high-crowned heads are seen to toss and glance; a glimpse of dazzling garden squares, and of sunshiny fountains coolly playing, and then, with a sweep, they drive up to the door, and the great bay horses stand still.

There is no need to open the door. It is already hospitably thrown back; and in the aperture stands a man less soberly clad than a butler, less floridly glorious than a footman. A man dressed all in virgin white, like a lily, a *débutante*, or a cricketer. On his feet are cricketing shoes, on his head brown hair, sheeny as only young hair ever is: on his cheeks and nose a coppery shining, which shows how, through the long summer day, the sun has been doing his wicked will upon him : in his eyes—the only part of his face to which the hot day's work has been unable to do any despite—a great young jollity and gladness. He is here then ! The ten days have begun. Only ten ! one, two, three, four, five, six, seven, eight, nine, ten !

She is out of the carriage, through the porch, away from the men-servants, in an inner hall before he gives her much greeting. There and then—they two being quite alone, a moderate richly-coloured light, filtering through the old and mellow dyes of a stained window, on their heads, and only dead stags' eyes staring glassily at them from the walls —she finds that both her hands are in his, and that he is saying to her most gravely, though with a smile :

"Welcome! welcome! welcome!" three times, and emphasising each repetition by a little pressure of her fingers. It would be pleasant to leave them in his, where, indeed, they feel most comfortably at home; she therefore instantly withdraws them. "Now at last I believe in your coming!" he cries, drawing a long glad breath. "I never did till now; there is something shifty and uncertain about you that one cannot reckon upon. I am afraid now to move my eyes away from you, lest when I looked again I should find

that you were half-way back to Portland
Villa !"

She smiles a little bitterly. "Am I then
so fond of Portland Villa ?" A pause. Her
eyes have been resting on the harmonious
muddle of the Turkey carpet ; she lifts them
to his face. "Where is Mrs. Wolferstan ?
am I not to be introduced to her ?"

"By-and-by, by-and-by !" he cries, with
impatient gaiety ; "you have hardly been introduced to me yet. *Apropos* of that, can
you conscientiously tell me, this time, that
you are glad to see me—not as a link,
mind,—not as a link !—but as myself, as
Anthony ?" She is silent. "I think you
are !" he says softly and slowly, "though
you would be torn asunder by wild horses
before you would own it. Have you made a
vow to keep my vanity at starving point ?
prison diet, bread and water, and very little
of that ?" Without waiting for her unready
answer, he goes on eagerly, "Then let me
tell you that I am glad enough for two, for

ten, for twenty! I am inconveniently, un-precedentedly, disagreeably glad!"

She looks up at him with a spirited smile. "Methinks, my lord, thou dost protest too much!" she says, altering the quotation.

"Ay, but I'll keep my word!" he cries quickly, catching it up where she has left it, and altering it too.

She laughs a little. "Where is Mrs. Wolferstan? If you will not find her for me, I shall be reduced to finding her for myself!"

"It would serve you right to let you try!" he says gaily. "Well! since you do not know when you are well off—" leading the way through empty rooms, along cool passages, up steps, down steps, till at length they stop before a door carefully protected by a heavy *portière.* Here they come to a standstill. "You have never seen her?" asks Anthony in a whisper, with his hand on the curtain.

"No."

"You have not the slightest idea what she is like?"

"Not the slightest," whispering too. "Is she like you?"

He smiles a little oddly. "I do not know. Does one ever know what oneself is like? She does not seem to me to have much resemblance to what I see in the glass!"

In another half moment they are in the room, and Joan is making her bow to Wolferstan's mother. The light is so dim that that which pervades a twilit cathedral at even-tide is garish in comparison. Rigorously closed *persiennes* outside the windows, lowered rose blinds inside, reduce the August sunshine to a minimum. Through the gloom she dimly sees an uncovered gold head, filleted with a pale pink ribbon, stooping towards her, and a civil, level, chilly voice saying:

"I hope you are not quite dead with the heat? I hope they have given you some tea!"

"Thank you! I had some before I set off."

"When I last saw you, you were only so

high," continues Mrs. Wolferstan, holding a thin pale hand heavily freighted with diamonds at a level of about a foot from the floor; "it was at Dering; you used to call me the pretty lady. Do you recollect? No?"

They are seated side by side on a lounge, with their backs carefully turned to the feeble light. Joan's eyes are fixed on her hostess: on the bright locks whose liberal gold has spread even over the parting; on the white muslin gown, generously open at the thin unyouthful neck (Joan's own milky throat is clothed up to the chin). She shakes her head. " I do not remember."

" But you did call me so, all the same!" repeats the other, her even voice taking a little sharpness of tone. A moment later, with recovered blandness : " Do you know I rather feel as if we had lured you here under false pretences ! Has Anthony told you we are quite, quite, quite alone ?"

Anthony nods. " It is true," he says laconically. " Do you mind ?"

"By-and-by," continues Mrs. Wolferstan, coldly smiling, "I hope we shall be a little more amusing. In about a week we may perhaps find some playfellows. Anthony dear," with a tart change of tone, "why will you always leave the door open? There comes in such a glare from the passage as I am sure must be blinding poor Miss Dering."

Anthony gets up docilely and shuts the door, successfully excluding thereby one small weak shaft of God's good light which was modestly trying to steal in; and again they sit in complete gloom. Ten minutes later, Mrs. Wolferstan having been summoned away to a colloquy with her maid, Anthony and Joan are again *tête-à-tête*. The moment that this is the case, he cries out in an exasperated voice:

"Why, in Heaven's name, could not you say that you recollected calling her the pretty lady? it would have made all the difference!"

"But I did not!" answers Joan, opening a pair of distressed blue eyes.

"Pooh!" he cries, laughing, yet vexed, "*qu'est ce que ça fait?* Such a fib would have been counted to you for righteousness!"

CHAPTER XVIII.

THE butler's practised hand has made its daily assault upon the Abbey gong, and the four people to whom its loud whirring has appealed are seated round the dinner-table. How delightful to be going to eat one's dinner without having had the whole bloom taken off the affair — without having had its existence forced upon one's notice for three preceding hours by the all pervasive smell of the rampant onion. There might not be such a bulb in existence for all that one perceives of it here.

Joan has made her entry into the dining-
room, with her hand on the back of a wheeled
chair, which is the nearest approach to taking
her into dinner of which the master of the
house is capable. For he, poor old gentleman, is in very indifferent repair, both of
mind and body, and is rolled in, nodding a
good deal and smiling foolishly, until snubbed
into gravity by an austere valet, who cuts up
his dinner and blows his nose for him.

"He only dines with us when we are alone,
of course!" says Mrs. Wolferstan in calm
apology; "but I thought you would not
mind!—no—it amuses him seeing strangers
and talking to them; he will answer you quite
rationally sometimes."

So now they are seated, while quiet-footed,
swift servants ply them with many palate-
tickling dishes. Joan thinks of Sarah labour-
ing round the table in creaky shoes and
smutty fingers, blowing the while like an
asthmatic grampus, and praises God for the
change in her circumstances. For the first

time since leaving Dering, she is dining.
Scores of times she has eaten—eaten from a
sense of duty, and to keep the wheels of the
machine going, but dined not once. Each
dish tastes more deliciously than its prede-
cessor; and after a long course of tepid water
and sour small beer, how pleasantly the Veuve
Clicquot, daintily sipped, stirs the blood in her
young veins!

"I am an epicure!" she says to herself in
shocked surprise; "good food or bad food
makes a perceptible difference in my happiness! to be, at my age, already a gourmet!"

In order to distract her attention from her
own gluttony, and relying on his wife's account
of his powers of conversation, she hazards a
timid observation to her host and neighbour
to the effect that "it is a fine day!" and is
much abashed at having her cheerfully meant
remark received with a burst of tears.

"Yes, it is a very fine day!" (sobbing).

In great discomfiture she looks across the
garden of late roses, that spreads in red pomp

and perfume over the table between them, at Anthony, who nods reassuringly, and says :

" It is all right ! he usually does it !"

She wishes that he would not nod ; he has a look of his father when he does.

" Were not you very sorry to leave Dering ?" asks Mrs. Wolferstan presently ; drawing still more deeply down the already large and opaque candle-shade over the candle nearest her ; " but I am silly—of course you were ! sweet old spot ! I am sure" (with a sigh) "no one can have pleasanter associations with it than I !"

Joan is silent. When her old home is mentioned she can depend upon neither voice nor eyes.

" Always something doing — something going on there !" pursues the other, her head poised on one side in pensive recollection ; " last time that I was there we got up some tableaux ; the very best of their kind, I think, that I have ever seen ! it was during the visit I was mentioning before dinner—the one that

you do not recollect!" (with a faintly resent-
ful intonation).

Joan is conscious that Anthony is looking
at her, with all his imploring soul thrown into
his eyes, across the table; that he is even
coughing with patent artificiality to attract
her attention to this glorious opportunity for
re-remembering the so unluckily forgotten
fact. But she lets it slip.

"In one, I remember," pursues Mrs. Wolferstan, with a half smile of complacent remi-
niscence, "I was the beggar's daughter of
Bethnal Green; bare feet, you know; and my
hair all loose about my shoulders" (touching
them with the tips of her fingers); "the
squire himself posed me, dear old man! of
course he was not old then! indeed *he* was
Cophetua."

"He was always so fond of pretty people!"
answers Joan, fixing her grave blue eyes upon
her hostess, and wondering whether, at that
distant epoch, the shoulders she mentions were
as bare of clothes and flesh, and as richly clad

in pearl powder as they now are ; " he liked
to have them about him."

"And I am sure that they returned the
compliment," answers Mrs. Wolferstan, with
brisk cordiality ; " at least I can answer for
myself, but I have always clung to my elders ;
it has been my way all my life ! I have never
cared for my contemporaries !"

Joan looks down at the plump quail on her
plate, with rose-reddened cheeks and bitten
lips, to repress the laughter rising within her
at the consciousness of the dumb pantomime
of applause and approbation which, invisibly
to any one but her, Anthony is going through
on the other side of the table, for her behoof.
Dinner is over and done with now : nothing
but its genial memory left ; and Joan stands
alone among the garden odours. Her hostess
has not accompanied her ; whether afraid that
the moonlight may bleach her gold hair, or
the night wind blow the pink from her cheeks,
is unknown.

So, by the fountain, with the slumberous

tumble of the far salt sea in her ears, and
with an enormously long slim shadow
stretching over the fine turf behind her,
Joan stands. The fountain is no longer
playing. Though the Tritons have their
mouths wide open, though the fat Cupids'
cheeks are still puffed out, no water issues
from their cold stone lips. In the basin the
water lies still as death, holding the moon
and the constellations on its heart. How
plainly mirrored is the fringe of ferns! each
frond so faithfully given back. Will she be
able to see her own face as clearly? Thriftily
lifting her gown, she kneels on the dewy turf;
and, leaning over the edge of the basin, peeps.
Her face is only a featureless blur. She dips
her hand into the water—then her wrist—
then almost all her arm. How pleasant to
feel the cold flood creeping round it! Then
she draws it out, and holds it aloft in the
moonbeams, admiring it. What a glorified
pearl-coloured limb! and how prettily the
shining wet drops race down it! Footsteps

make small noise on turf; and before she suspects it, some one is beside her. Ashamed of being found out in an employment so babyish and so vain, she rises hastily, and, trying covertly to wipe her arm on her pocket-handkerchief without being detected, cries out:

" Did you ever see anything so long as my shadow? it is running up the house! it has reached the second story!"

" It is trying to get in at my windows," answers Anthony, for it is he.

" Those are my windows!"

" Are they? But you need not be conceited about it; mine is quite as tall!" (moving towards her, and standing so close beside her that their two shadows unite and blend into a single whole), " see! we are one!" (deepening the meaning of the trifling jesting words by the emphasis of his moonlit eyes).

" But we can very soon be two again!" cries Joan briskly, moving away from him, and turning her face towards the house.

" You are not going in ?" he says in a tone of strong disapprobation ; getting ahead of her, and backing slowly before her ; " until I came you were good for another hour's moon-gazing !"

" Another hour ! no—another half hour ! perhaps—yes !" (with a fine smile).

" Am I a fog or a miasma, that I should drive you in ?" he cries in an offended voice. She laughs lightly, yet restlessly ; and the eyes that, against their will, meet his are full of an uneasy distrust.

" I do not know !   I am not quite sure that you are not !"

They are standing still again.   Joan has stopped perforce, seeing that one other backward step will precipitate Anthony into the flamy depths of a geranium bed.   Above their heads a bright half moon—no crescent —an honest half, as if it had been accurately sliced in two ; below their feet the freshness of the hoary dew.

" May I ask, are you apt to catch cold ?"

23—2

She shakes her head.

" Have you a delicate throat ?"

" No."

" A weak chest ?"

" No."

" Rickety lungs ?"

She laughs a little.

" To save you the pain of further catechism, I will tell you that, as far as I know, I am perfectly sound everywhere !"

"Do you like fresh air?" he goes on eagerly ; " because if so, let me tell you that indoors every window is tightly closed—every shutter rigorously barred ! Do you like conversation ? you will have to do without it ! my mother is asleep and dislikes to be waked ; do you like light and occupation ? you will get neither ! it is one of our manners and customs to grope through our evenings in Egyptian gloom !"

She is silent.

" Not convinced yet ?" he cries in a tone of impatient astonishment, but half feigned ;

"then go! buy dearly the experience that I was willing to give you for nothing!"

But with the permission to go, she seems to lose the inclination.

"What time is it?" she asks, after thinking a moment; "take out your watch! I have not one." Then, as he obeys her, and they both stoop over the little disk, "There!" she says, placing one small moonlit finger firmly on a figure on the dial-plate, "I will stay till then!"

"A beggarly quarter of an hour!" says the young man, grumbling; "what can one say in a quarter of an hour?"

"If one speaks quickly one can say an immense number of sentences!" answers Joan demurely; "thousands I should think; had not you better begin at once?"

But he seems in no hurry to comply with her suggestion. Slowly, and in a luxury of silence, they step side by side through the windless night. Above their heads, in the suave far sky, God's countless noiseless

armies are all awake and ashine. Thin
trails of silvered clouds are flung hither and
thither across the deep blue space. One is
even thrown, like a lawny veil, about the
moon's face; but it is so transparent, so luminous, that she looks through it with hardly
lessened lustre.

Joan's head is thrown back; and her eyes
and all her face are lifted upwards, seeking,
among the numberless battalions of the unknown, the few familiar faces of her shining
friends.

"Have you finished counting the stars?"
asks Anthony presently, breaking the silence.

"Not quite!" (laughing a little, but not
changing her position).

"There is no hurry!" says the young man
affably; "if you are content, so am I; I am
looking at you at my leisure. I am not at
all sure that I do not like looking at you
better than talking to you; your face is so
far gentler than your speech; I am sorry for
your own sake that you cannot see at this

moment how delicately and neatly your profile is cut out against the sky !"

If he had meant to bring her look down to earth again, he could not have taken a better course. In a moment the features he praises have come back to their usual level, and are turned with youthful severity towards him.

" Have you forgotten our agreement ?" she asks, with soft austerity ; " have you forgotten that I am a *man* friend—an honest bon camarade to be treated with rational plain speaking, not to be used as a whetstone for banal civilities ?"

He nods gravely.

" I have not forgotten, but you must allow that there is a different code of morals and manners for sunshine and moonshine—all day you shall be a man—there ! can anything be fairer ? and as soon as the moon rises, you shall become again a woman—a most womanly woman !" slowly drawing out the last words with a lagging fondness, while his eyes plunge

with a passionate audacity of admiration into
the chaste deeps of hers. Under that look
she turns her small sleek head about restlessly,
and trembles a little as one afraid.

"I am sure that the time is up!" she says
uneasily; "I am sure that it is more than a
quarter of an hour—let me look for myself!"

He takes out his watch, and holding it up
at some little distance from her for the space
of an instant, hastily returns it to his pocket.

"Ten minutes more!" he says promptly;
"only five gone—I thought so!"

"A very long five minutes!" says Joan
suspiciously.

They have seated themselves on a wooden
bench under a tree. From an island of black
shade they look out upon a sea of white moonlight. Around them is the perfect stillness
that the rich man can make about his
dwelling; no noise of rolling wheels, or of
drunken men uproariously singing, which has
so often of late been Joan's lullaby; no noise,
save only the sea's far speech, its comfortable

voice speaking coolly through the sultry night.

"There is one great want in the English language," says Anthony presently, with apparent irrelevancy; "has it ever struck you? One has to employ the same pronoun to one's sweetheart and one's laundress. One says to the first, 'You are a darling;' and to the second, 'You have not put enough starch in my collars.' Ought not there to be a difference? Why does not one say 'thou' to the people one loves? I have a great longing to call you 'thou' to-night."

In the heart of this thick-clad tree it is too dark to see clearly, but his voice sounds dangerously moved, and Joan has a dim impression of young and flashing eyes. She laughs coldly and lightly.

"Why do not you, then? Pray do if you like; I am sure I have no objection."

"You have dried up all inclination," he cries angrily, retiring into the farthest corner of the bench, out of which he had before been making cautious and stealthy advances like a horned snail out of its shell. "As long as I live I shall never wish to call you 'thou' again! if there were any colder pronoun than 'you,' I should make a point of employing it."

She laughs again mockingly.

"He, she, they, it; I give you your choice of them all. I will answer to any one of them."

As she speaks she rises, and, leaving his side, steps softly forth into the moonlight again. They have left the great main garden, with its terraces, its million bedding plants, its ingenious unlovely flower mosaics. They are in the seclusion of a little ancient parterre that has survived from the olden time. Here formal bed box-edged answers to formal bed. Here the yew-peacock still keeps his shape; here many well-smelling out-of-fashion dwellers in old gardens have taken refuge, watched over by a quiet garden god done in stone, while around a tall trellis, over flung by clematis, up-climbed by roses, profuse almost as June's, make a high close wall.

"We will come here every night," says Anthony, following her, and standing by her side beneath the trellis; "every night I will gather you a bunch of roses." As he speaks he stretches out his right arm far and high, and plucking bloom after bloom, gives them one by one to her. "Here is one creamy-white like your throat; here is another warmly red as one of your ears is now; which ear is it, the left? ah, then some one is speaking ill of you! what a ruffian he must be! here is another brightly pink as your nostrils were to-day, when the sun shone through them."

"And this?" cries Joan in a mischievous voice, making a snatch at a deep yellow rose which droops just above her head—a rose golden-hearted as the yolk of an egg—"which of my features is this like?"

He stops abruptly, and his arm drops to his side.

" I give you up," he cries in a disgusted voice ; " I have done with you ; for warping, searing, withering, drying up all a man's holiest impulses, I will back you against any woman in Great Britain or Ireland."

" It is your own fault," says Joan, dropping her rallying tone, and relapsing into gravity ; " how many times have I told you that I dislike personal remarks ?"

" At least a thousand !" replies the young man coolly ; " and I foresee that you will have to tell me so a thousand times more ! what ! one may go into any hysterics of admiration that one chooses over a mountain, a sunset, a glacier ; and before the loveliest thing God ever made, one must stand dumb —mum chance !"

" But you do not see me for the first time," objects Joan, mollified in spite of herself, and smiling slightly ; " perhaps I might forgive you, if my beauty " (with a little ironical accent) " burst upon you to-night with the shock of a surprise, but by now

you surely have had time to grow used
to it !"

" Have I ?" answers the young man with
trenchant emphasis; "when, pray? when have
I ever had a really good long leisurely look at
or talk with you ? a skimped half-hour here—a
meagre ten minutes there—are all the pay I
have had for the long and many hours which
I have spent sitting on hard stiles and
dodging behind prickly hedges to catch a
sight of you ! you do not believe me !" (noting
the gentle scepticism of her slow moonlit
smile). " I give you my word of honour that
I know every rung of that ladder stile that
leads into the Helmsley Road as well as I
know my own features ! I could tell you
how many bricks there are in each wall of
Portland Villa; I know the shape of the
chimney-pots far better than I know the
shape of my own nose !" Again she smiles,
with a small disbelieving head-shake, while
her eyes droop to the fine drenched sward at
her feet, and her right hand slowly waves

about her dewy rose bunch. "And if I came to call," pursues the young man, pricked into greater heat and emphasis by her incredulity, "you know as well as I do, that I came as often as decency would permit, and several times oftener; what profit had I? Once, after I left, I counted the remarks you had made during my visit; they were five; and of them, three were 'Yes,' and one was 'No.'"

"Other people were talking," answers Joan apologetically; "you know that it is only among rooks or geese that it is considered good manners for every one to speak at once."

Anthony is silent, but it is clearly not the silence of conviction.

"You know," continues Joan deprecatingly, "that to them it is a great treat to talk to you."

" *To them!*" repeats Anthony, with a short and rather offended laugh; "thank you for the emphasis!"

"They so seldom meet a man of your class —of your type," pursues the girl, not heeding his interruption ; "and—and—of course they do not know—they do not understand !" A moment later, with painfully hot cheeks and quickened breath : "Apropos of that, I have a favour to ask of you ; now that we are alone I must not lose the opportunity ; I want" (lifting two meek troubled eyes to his expectant face)—"I want to make you promise never to come and call upon me again."

"*Never to come and call upon you again!*"

"I know," continues Joan, beginning to speak very fast, and still looking at him humbly yet steadily—"I know that you mean it in all kindness and civility, but if you knew" (with an unmistakable accent of sincerity)—"if you knew how I hate your visits !"

"Thank you."

"If you knew how my heart sinks when the door-bell rings for fear that it may be you !"

"Thank you!"

"I grow hot, I grow cold, I choke!" cries the girl, with an accent of deepening excitement; "when I see their unnecessary overdone effusiveness — their mistaken joy in greeting you—when I watch you with difficulty hiding your mirth! no—do not mistake me" (seeing that he is about to interrupt her), "you do hide it, at least they do not see it; but I!—how can I help it? I divine it, and it suffocates me!"

Anthony is silent; an uncomfortable scarlet silence. Fain would he asseverate that the sight of the Misses Moberley and their mamma has no perceptible effect on his gravity, but the words stick in his throat. Did he swear this till he was black in the face, he knows that she would not believe him.

"Do not think that I blame you!" continues Joan, in a dejected tone, while her unoccupied hand idly strays among the gray-green sprays and tendrils of the bowery clematis; "were I in your place, no doubt I should not be able to keep my countenance so well as you do ; but, things being as they are, they being my very near relatives, my closest kin, you may fancy that it is hardly amusement that I feel !"

Anthony turns away, writhing involuntarily as the redundant form and over-blown face of Bell Moberley rise in awful distinctness before his mind's eye. "If this appalling fact be true, why, in Heaven's name, should she put it into words ?"

"As you know," continues Joan, sighing a little, while her downcast eyes still stray sadly over the numberless little white flowers and the downy fluff of the clematis—"as you know, mine is not a particularly sweet lot ! well—when I tell you that each of your visits pours an additional drop of gall into my cup, I am sure that I need say nothing further to persuade you to leave them off !"

She stops : her voice, grown a little tremulous, dies into silence. Nothing breaks the suave dumbness of the night. A very light air has arisen, and is gently swinging the heavy-folded roses and playing over the garden god's cold limbs, the girl's soft face, and the man's troubled one.

As they so stand, Joan resolutely waiting for the answer which Anthony is equally resolved not to give, the stable clock breaks upon the silence with eleven clear slow strokes.

" Eleven !" cries Joan, starting ; " why does it strike eleven ? it must be an hour too fast !" Anthony does not answer, save by a guilty expression of face. " What time is it by your watch ? no—I will see for myself this time."

He produces it with some reluctance. The hour hand points to eleven.

" It was a pious fraud !" says the young man apologetically, but laughing ; " the end justifies the means !"

But the last half of his sentence is addressed to himself or the trellis, for Joan has taken

to her heels, and quick as a rabbit is scudding
between the high box hedges back to the
house.

✻　　✻　　✻　　✻　　✻

Half an hour later she is standing in her
bedroom, lost in honest admiration of the
large white bed, the spouted jugs and un-
cracked basins, the whole and healthy carpet,
and the safe-legged dependable chairs.

" Half a day—a twentieth part of my visit
is over !" she says aloud ; " there are only nine
and a half days left !"

CHAPTER XIX.

FOR the first time for weeks Joan lies all night in cool, deep, blessed sleep, unvexed by miserable hot tossings, by weary waiting for the dawdling clock strokes as they mark the passage of the sultry night; nor is she awoke by the fierce sun, who is kept at bay by careful awnings and ample blinds. Her drowsy blue eyes first open on the unwonted luxury of a cup of tea brought to her bedside by a trim house-maid, upon whose cheeks no smuts have found a home, and whose gown is absolutely undecorated by rents or grease.

Joan rises gaily with a springy feeling of youth and prosperity at her heart, walks with childish enjoyment barefooted on the thick soft carpet, revels in the plentiful hot water; and, in utter jollity of mind, makes faces at herself in the glass, wherein eyes, nose, and mouth are faithfully rendered, undisturbed by any perverting crack. She has put on her gown now—her hot black gown—all her gowns are hot and heavy and black.

"I look as if I had been dipped in the ink-bottle up to my neck," she says discontentedly. As she speaks her eyes fall on Anthony's roses blooming in a china bowl upon her dressing-table. She takes them out one by one. "This is the one that is like my throat; this is the one that is like my ear; this is the one that is like my nose— my nostrils, I mean." She sighs a little, and puts them back again. "It would elate him," she says, "and it must be the object of my life to depress him." So saying, and shaking her head, she takes the one yellow rose which she herself had plucked over night in order to insult her admirer, and fastens it in the breast of her gown. Whilst so occupied a gong sounds. "In any house I have ever visited," she says to herself, "there have always been two, sometime three, gongs. The first means nothing; the second means prayers; the third means breakfast: I will wait for the third."

In pursuance of this resolve she sits down on the window-seat (alas! that window-seats are so nearly extinct!), and resting her elbows on the sill, takes her face in both hands, and leans out in leisurely enjoyment of the new morning's well-scented splendours. But by-and-by, as no second gong either sounds or appears to have any intention of sounding, and as many clocks with voices small and big, slow and fast, announce to her from different parts of the house that it is ten o'clock, she rises and goes downstairs.

There is no one in the large sitting-hall but Anthony, who, lounging in an oak chair,

whence he commands a full view of the stair-
case, is looking up every minute from his
Times with quick impatient eyes "gray as
glasse." When at length Joan comes stepping sedately down, her little pointed shoes
cautiously clacking against the low slippery
steps, and one small milk-white hand sliding
down the old black banister, he hastily throws
away his paper, and comes eagerly to meet
her.

" You will never be ' healthy, wealthy, and
wise,' " he says. " Do you know that it is
ten o'clock ; not by my watch" (laughing),
" but by Greenwich time. I began to be
afraid that you had gone back to Portland
Villa. How are you ? Shall we come to
breakfast ?"

" Had not we better wait for Mrs. Wolferstan ?" suggests Joan, hanging back.

" We should have to wait some time"
(laughing again). " She never appears before
one o'clock."

" And your father ?" in a rather troubled

voice; for will not the presence of even a
foolishly tearful, foolishly mirthful, old imbe-
cile be better than nothing as a protection
against the dangers of this apparently never-
ending still beginning *tête-à-tête.*'

"My father breakfasts in his own room,"
replies Anthony rather shortly, beginning to
look a little restive.

There is no help for it. " Fate is against
me," she says to herself, and so, without
further objection, follows him into the dining-
room.

He sends away the servants, and asks her
whether she will pour out the tea. They sit
opposite to each other in quasi-conjugal duet.
It is true that at first the urn interposes its
large body between them, but, by a crafty and
gradual shifting of himself and his plate,
Anthony by-and-by obviates the difficulty,
and commands an unintercepted view of his
companion. It is in the morning that youth
and complexion tell the most; at night
any dingy skin can look white; under the

benevolent rule of wax-candles any human buttercup passes for a lily, but not so when the downright sun is searching into the weak places of human countenances, and drawing his absolute line of demarcation between foul and fair. Joan's skin is as clear and fine as privet flowers; you might look at it through a microscope.

"We have dined together," says Anthony presently, neglecting his grill and leaning meditatively on his elbow, "and we have lunched together."

"Yes, we have lunched together," replies Joan, shuddering a little at the recollection of Sarah and the melted butter.

"But," continues Anthony, "this is the first time that we have ever breakfasted together."

"Yes."

As he speaks her thoughts fly back to that day in the wood months ago when he had so earnestly impressed upon her mind the weariness that he would feel in sitting opposite the

same woman every day at breakfast. How
soon would he grow weary of sitting opposite
her? He is not weary yet, apparently. She
wishes that he would retire behind the urn
again.

"Now how shall we lay out our day?"
cries the young man by-and-by, when breakfast being at length, to Joan's relief, ended.
They stand again together in the hall. "You
have absolutely nothing to do; I have absolutely nothing to do; let us enjoy ourselves."

The jollity of his tone is catching; Joan's
eyes sparkle with a temperate hilarity.

"Shall we? by all means!"

"But how?" continues Anthony reflectively. "I know a good many things that
you do not like, but very few that you do.
You like the sea? shall we have a boat and
go out dredging?"

"Certainly not."

"Shall we ride?"

"Too hot."

"Shall we play lawn tennis?"

" Too hot."

" Shall we go into the kitchen-garden and eat plums ?"

" At once ?" (lifting her eyebrows). " We should never come out again alive."

" I have it !" says Anthony, with an air of inspiration. "There is a lake up among the hills that you have never seen—that I think you have never seen. I will drive you up there in my T-cart ; we will fish all day, and come back in the cool of the evening. I will go and tell them to put up some luncheon at once."

He is half-way to the door, when her eager voice overtakes and stops him.

" Impossible ! quite impossible !"

" Why impossible ?"

For a moment she does not answer, save by the slightly deeper dye that stains the fine grain of her cool cheeks, and her eyes drop to the spotted leopard skin at her feet. Then she looks up, and says gently yet seriously, " You made me uncivil last night ;

you must not make me uncivil again this morning. I had rather make no plans until I see Mrs. Wolferstan."

"Then you will waste half the day," in a nettled tone. She is silent. "You might just as well be back at Portland Villa !" (with rising exasperation).

She looks up with a softly conciliatory smile. "Shall I go back ?"

But Colonel Wolferstan has his plan a very great deal too much at heart to be diverted from it by a smile.

"We should catch nothing !" pursues Joan persuasively, looking out through the open windows at the absolute turquoise of the heavens. "Look at the sky ! and there has been no rain for weeks !"

"Who wants to catch anything ?" asks the young man, laughing petulantly; "of course we should not. I never caught anything there in my life ! I do not believe that there is anything to catch ; but we should get well away from everybody for the whole day.

You have no conception of the loneliness of the place : not a soul ever goes there—we might perhaps see a heron or a carrion crow."

" It would be hardly worth while going such a long way to see only one carrion crow, would it ?" says Joan, with a fine smile.

He makes a gesture of impatience. " You will not, then ?"

" Not to-day !" tempering her refusal by the blue sweetness of her eyes.

" It is, perhaps, your last chance !" (with a vexed laugh). "I may never invite you again."

She shrugs a little, and also smiles again.

" No ? Then I must imagine the carrion crow !" He walks to the door, but this time with no elated hurry. " That is your last word ?"

" My last word."

He disappears. She watches him with serenity, feeling sure that the door will shortly open to re-admit him. But in this she is mistaken, for time passes, but he does

not return. She watches the hands creep
round the clocks' faces, and the pendulums
tiresomely swinging. In solitude the hours
pass ; a peaceful harmonious solitude indeed,
soothed by sweet smells and the sight of
pretty things ; unbroken by the loud wrang-
ling of underbred servants in the kitchen, or
the shrill peevish jars of Mrs. Moberley and
Bell, yet still solitude. As he said, she might
just as well be back at Portland Villa.

All the clocks, even the slowest, have
struck one, and there is yet no sign of her
hostess, when Anthony at length reappears.

" I hope it will not inconvenience you," he
says in a rather formal voice, walking over
to the window nearest him, " but I am afraid
I must pull down all the blinds ; my mother
cannot bear a strong light. Do you mind ?"

" Not in the least!" replies Joan with
alacrity, rising and obligingly helping in the
sacrilegious task of shutting out all the warm
rainbow-tinted outside glories, and reducing
the apartment to a uniform pink gloom.

"There is no accounting for tastes, is there?" says the young man dryly, when their task is completed; then, in a rather hesitating tone, "Would you mind—do you think you could manage to let her imagine that you *liked* it?"

Having said this he rather hastily goes away again. Shortly afterwards Mrs. Wolferstan appears. Rome was not built in a day, nor is Mrs. Wolferstan built in an hour; but now, at length, with every ravage repaired and every breach made good, she enters.

"I am so glad to see that you do not share Anthony's mania for a *glare*," she says, looking round with satisfaction on the rosy false twilight; "that, like me, you enjoy a subdued light!" Joan smiles involuntarily. "As for Anthony," continues his mother, "he would live in a glass-house if he could; he sleeps with his bed facing the window, and all the blinds drawn up. Can you conceive such a thing?"

Joan can conceive it, for it is the course of conduct that she herself always pursues; but, mindful of Colonel Wolferstan's request, she holds her peace.

"You will not mind my saying so, dear," continues Mrs. Wolferstan a moment later, while her bistred eyes take in the wintry blackness of her young guest's *tout-ensemble*, " but your gown—nothing can be nicer I am sure—but is not it a little *warm* ?"

" Frightfully !" answers Joan, laughing, " but it is the coolest I have. All my clothes are adapted for a polar winter !"

" Would you be angry " (putting her head slightly on one side) "if I were to offer to lend you one of my little morning wrappers—like *this*" (holding out for inspection the airy fabric of her cobwebby *peignoir*); " they are the comfort of my life; I *live* in them. We are as nearly as possible the same height, I should say " (leading the young girl before a pier-glass)—" we must be measured—Anthony must measure us; and not unlike in figure either !" (drawing up her thin neck, and, with obvious dishonesty, standing on tiptoe).

Joan is silent.

"When I married," says her companion, moving away from the glass again, "I could span my waist with my two hands—so !"

"Could you really ?" says Joan, smiling. "I should find some difficulty in doing that."

As she speaks she puts her hands on her waist, and joining the finger tips at the back, laughs to see the very considerable space that parts from each other her small thumbs.

"I believe it was an unusual case," says Mrs. Wolferstan modestly. "Of course they said that I laced tight ; the fact was that I wore no corset at all !"

"No ?"

"Well" (with a sigh), "I am afraid I must not let you make me idle !—letters, you know, and our post goes out early. So sorry to leave you alone ! you do not mind ? No ? That is like me—nothing I enjoy so much as my own society !—' never less alone than when alone.' I am like that. Well, *au revoir!* till luncheon-time."

Nodding and smiling she disappears, and Joan is alone again.

These, then, are all the thanks that she gets for her wasted morning, all the pay that rewards her sacrifice to the conventionalities. Unable to read by the poor modicum of light left, and afraid to pull up the blinds, she creeps behind one of them ; and kneeling on the floor, lays her book on the window-sill, and begins to read. While so occupied she hears the door-handle again turn, and peeping out from her retreat, sees Anthony looking uncertainly in—half of his body in the strong white sunlight from the hall, half in a rose-pink bath.

He really must not be allowed to go away again.

"You look so odd and pink," she cries out gaily.

The remark decides him, for he comes in and shuts the door.

"The same to you," he answers, advancing towards her; "you will find that we mostly look pink here—*nous autres!* it is a little way we have. Mother not down yet?"

"She came in here about a quarter of an hour ago."

"And went away again?"

"Almost immediately."

A malicious smile curves the young man's handsome lips, even more than nature has done it for him; lightens also in his clear steel-coloured eyes.

"This is the way in which the Goddess Ydgrun, or Mother Grundy, mostly rewards her votaries, and you see that you might just as well have been obliging after all."

"Just as well."

"But for you," continues Anthony incisively, sitting down on a small stool in front of her, also behind the blind, "we should now have been reclining under a large gray rock, side by side, eating pâté de foie gras."

Joan shakes her head.

" I should not ; I hate foie gras."

" You would have been eating something else then ; what would you have been eating? *I* should have been eating foie gras."

" Yes ?"

" In the brook at our feet—did I mention that there is a brook as well as a lake—a brook ice-cold on the hottest summer day—a bottle of champagne."

" *A* bottle !" interrupts Joan playfully, raising her eyebrows ; " why not a dozen ?— we may as well have a carouse !"

" By all means ; in the brook, then, a dozen bottles of champagne are standing up to their necks ; we ourselves couched like ruminating cattle on the heather, which, as you are perhaps aware, is now in full flower ; above our heads the birds are carolling their little hearts out."

" Excuse my interrupting you," says Joan gravely ; " but they do not sing a note now."

" No more they do ! above our heads, then—"

"The one carrion crow is hovering," cries the girl, breaking into a laugh, "croaking frightfully."

" Crows do not croak !"

" Is hovering over our heads, then, in utter silence, more alarming than any sound he could make."

" We will not quarrel over details," says Anthony magnanimously ; "and since you own that you might just as well have been obliging—you *do* own it, do not you ?"

She nods.

" Yes, I own it."

" And when next I exert myself to make a little plan—"

" I will hasten to meet it !" answers Joan, her blue eyes dancing.

" Come into the garden," says Anthony ; " we will seal our reconciliation with plums."

CHAPTER XX.

F Joan's visit a whole week has gone; and though the proposed duration of her stay is now increased from ten days to a fortnight, yet there is no denying the fact that even so a full half is already over. Seven such good days! Can the next seven be as good? Hardly. Bell's envious prophecy has been fulfilled to the letter. She has had Anthony all to herself. And now the latter half of the prediction is to be accomplished. To-day the house is to fill with "stylish London people." At the thought Joan's heart sinks. They may be good—these seven

new days—but certainly their goodness will be of a different character.

Her mind strays lovingly back over the gone week—her own one week that none can now ever take from her. Breakfast *tête-à-tête* with Anthony; a stroll between the great yew hedges with Anthony; rowing on the calm brown river between the banks of flowered bulrushes with Anthony; walking on the firm gold of the sea sands and gathering long-haired sea-tang with Anthony; eating mulberries with Anthony; quarrelling with Anthony; forgiving Anthony; gazing at the planets and the milky way, and often forgetting to look at them, with Anthony. Adam and Eve in Paradise could hardly have had a more absolute duet. For a whole week Joan's biography has been the biography of Anthony; Anthony's biography has been the biography of Joan. How will it be with her life when the Anthony element has been eliminated from it? It is as well to look at these things now and then! For a whole week no one has sought to come between, to interrupt or balk them. Not even Anthony's mother has manifested the smallest surprise or alarm at the unceasing nature of their *tête-à-têtes.*

" It is my insignificance that protects me !" Joan says to herself bitterly; " I am too entirely undesirable to be even feared, or else" (smiling bitterly) " it is his way !— no doubt it is his way !"

For the first time she has spent a morning without Anthony, and has made the agreeable discovery of how leaden-footed such a morning has become. It has walked away as if it had wooden clogs on. She has passed the hours by the side of Mrs. Wolferstan in the barouche, rolling into Helmsley and back again, along the well-known road where she has so often tiredly plodded in most unwilling pursuit of the military. Every step seems marked by the memory of some mean humiliation or paltry pain.

With a shudder of distaste she looks at

Portland Villa as they pass—Portland Villa
—from whose windows, for a wonder, no heads
are seen protruding; at whose gate no army
of tight-curled bellicose dogs is drawn up in
battle array. This phenomenon is speedily
accounted for; when, a little farther along
the road, they come upon a walking party of
five persons, whose advent is heralded by
their laughter some time before they come
in sight. The procession is headed by Bell
and the regimental doctor, who have apparently been playfully exchanging hats; for,
as the carriage approaches, there is a friendly
scuffle between them to regain each their own
natural head-gear. Diana and Micky follow,
less playful perhaps, but still agreeably
mirthful; and the rear is brought up by
Mrs. Moberley, who follows swainless, half
of her gown trailing two yards behind her in
the dust, which envelops her in a sort of
choky nimbus, and the other half kilted so
unintentionally, unnaturally high as to give
to view a great deal of ankle and a broad

burst boot, from which most of the buttons are missing.

"Would you like to stop?" asks Mrs. Wolferstan, becoming aware of this remarkable spectacle, and honestly trying to make her words sound as little dissuasive as possible; "no?—well, perhaps the sun is rather trying when one is standing still. I have a horror of *coup de soleil*, so I see have you!"

As she speaks she gives a civil general bow to the hot-faced dusty-footed *cortége*, and they roll on. It is clear that this manœuvre is unexpected by the Moberley party, who have drawn themselves up in a row by the side of the road, in evident expectation of a colloquy. Diana, indeed, has slunk a little behind, looking shamefaced yet excited; but Bell is well to the front, and has already begun a sentence in her resonant loud voice. Micky has taken off his hat, and is waving it with more than his usual martial ease and assured familiarity; and the doctor is all one friendly grin from ear to ear. Guessing their disappointment,

Joan leans out to nod and smile with anxious emphasis, and is thus in a position clearly to see the way in which all their jaws have dropped, and the wrathy astonishment painted on three out of the five warmly-tinted faces; viz. on Mrs. Moberley's, Bell's, Micky's. She sinks back on the cushions with a feeling of keen mortification and suffering.

"They think that I am giving myself airs!" she says to herself; "I who am indebted to them for daily bread, but oh! I could not— I could not have borne it!"

She is shocked to find how much even a week has blunted her recollection of them. They are so much, *much* worse than she had remembered them; especially, oh! most especially, Micky. Even Mr. Brown's legs are longer, and his tail curls less than she had any idea of. The impression of the rencontre lives with her all through the rest of the drive, and embitters it. She cannot shake it off. Not even the sight of Anthony, eager-eyed, awaiting them under the great stone porch; not even the strongly-accented pressure of his hand, as he helps her out of the carriage, can quite dissipate it. There are only six and a half more days on which hers can meet his. After that it will be Micky's, Micky's, always Micky's; Micky, whose coarse hot hand ever holds hers so much longer and tighter than it wishes to be held. Later on, even when they are sitting side by side in their wonted place in the warm green silence of the sleepy wood, the impression still lasts, still stings. It is even deepened and complicated by a new and yet more unpleasant one, left by a few words of Mrs. Wolferstan's.

"What restless people you are!" she cries, as she sees the two friends preparing to steal out after luncheon together, and speaking in a sharper tone than Joan has yet heard her employ; and with a keener look in her stained and bistred eyes than she has yet observed in them; "how unlike me! give me a book—play, poem, essay, what you will—and I never wish to stir from hour's end to hour's end;

while you, even in the dog days, you must always be on the move—on the move!"

"It is cooler in the wood than in the house," says Joan gently yet persistently; feeling that she will not part company from her last chance of a *tête-à-tête* without a death struggle.

"In the wood!" repeated Mrs. Wolferstan, raising herself on her white muslin elbow, and looking pettishly at her son. "Is it possible, Anthony, that you are going to take Miss Dering all through that long tangle of grass and nettles and brushwood?"

"There is no long tangle," replies Anthony sulkily; "and even if there were, it would be as dry as tow this weather."

"And I am well shod," says the girl, with a deprecating smile, holding up a small shoe for inspection.

"Oh, we see that you have a pretty foot, my dear," says the elder woman, with a rather *aigre-doux* smile. "Are you an Andalusian? Can water run under it without wetting it?

People used to be very absurd about my foot once upon a time : I remember one man telling me that he wondered how any grown-up body could be supported on such a tiny pedestal. My bootmaker asked leave to exhibit one of my little boots in a glass-case in his shop window !—too silly, was not it ?"

Protected by this fire of complacent reminiscences they move towards the door; but before they are safely through it they are again arrested.

"You will be back in good time, Anthony ! you will not be late ?"

"Does the tocsin of the dinner-gong ever fail to find us in our accustomed places ?" asks Anthony impatiently.

"The dinner-gong ! I must beg you to return long before then ! Lalage's train arrives at 5.50."

"*Après ?*"

"*Après !* well" (in a tone at once fretful and imperative), "I must request that you are back in time to receive her ; she will quite expect it. Do you think " (with a little dry laugh) " that I imagine she is coming to visit me ? *pas si bête !*"

They have escaped at last; but it is not the same thing as if they had got away ten minutes earlier.

In a dead stupid silence they take their way to the greenwood depths. A great stretch of sun-roasted gardens intervenes between them and their refuge. He has unfurled a large green sunshade, which he holds over her head. It entails such a proximity that they are almost leaning against one another; but still they do not speak. Her eyes are on the burnt grass; his are staring out straight before him. They have been silent before now when together, but it was not the same sort of silence.

They have reached the wood. The sunshade is no longer needed. As soon as its connecting influence is withdrawn they insensibly walk a little farther from each other. They have passed along the winding walk and reached the well-known retired seat : no ornamental chair with writhen legs, but a simple log of wood, over which the mosses have bountifully spread themselves. Side by side they sit, still wordless. High above them the Scotch firs lay their grave dark heads together, and keep out the sun; at their feet is the veined and patterned ivy; around them a great spread of brambles, with the arch of their mighty crimson stalks and the plenty of their berries; a tangle of greenery, just touched here and there into early fire by the impatient finger of Autumn.

" Lalage !" " 5.50 !" " *Pas si bête !*"

These phrases are buzzing and dinning in Joan's ears, drowning the trumpeting of the loud gnats and the twitter of the happy finches. At last she speaks, without preface, abruptly :

" Who is Lalage ?"

He does not answer for a moment. He is plucking sour little wild strawberries, and eating them; then he speaks in a slow dreamy tone :

"Lalage is—Lalage !"

"She has a surname, I suppose ?"

"I suppose she has !" (absently).

"*Suppose!*"

"What am I saying?" cries the young man, rousing himself. "Of course she has! Beauchamp — that is her name ! Lalage Beauchamp. L. B.—I ought to know her initials" (making a face as he throws away his last tart strawberry).

"Beauchamp ! oh !"

"Lalage, Lalage !" repeats Anthony slowly, and draggingly, as he clasps one knee with both hands and throws his eyes upwards to the tree tops and the blue chinks of heaven between; "did you ever hear such a name to give a sober Christian woman ? Does not it give one a tipsy, demoralised, Bacchic idea ?"

She makes no comment. Her tongue

seems tied up with a tight uncomfortable
string.

"Will you hear the tale of Lalage?" asks
Anthony presently, stretching out his hand
to gather a bit of over-blown cranes bill,
with its little pink stalks and long sharp
noses; "there *is* a tale about her, as you
no doubt perceive. I know that you will
never be easy until you hear it; and as for
me, you know that I always have a diseased
pleasure in relating to you anything that tells
to my own disadvantage. Shall I?"

"Yes."

She adds nothing to this short affirmative.

"Well then—please attend—this is really
worth listening to. The last time I saw her
—at least to speak to—I was weeping copi-
ously, and following her round the room on
my knees—there!" He is not looking at her;
he is looking away from her, perhaps purposely, and she blesses him for it. For the
moment she feels that her face has passed
beyond her control, and that she has as

little power over its muscles as she has over those of his. "Have I quite taken your breath away?" he asks, still without turning his head towards her, but peeping surreptitiously at her out of the corner of one anxious eye.

"Rather!" she answers, speaking as one that pants a little from being carried too quickly through the air, or suddenly plunged into the sea. Then making an effort over herself: "You were quite young, perhaps?—a boy?"

He shakes his head. "I wish I could conscientiously say that I was in petticoats; but I am afraid that I was quite as big as I am now. I wore her Majesty's uniform; I had cut all my teeth; I was twenty-two years of age. No! there were no palliating circumstances."

"Followed her round the room on your knees," says Joan, repeating his former words in a stupid parrot tone, and without the faintest sense of that ludicrousness in the

26—2

situation which would have struck her so keenly had the case been that of any one else; "and—and—what was she doing?"

"She was laughing immoderately," replies Anthony, a sort of mirth curling the corners of his own handsome lips at the recollection. "Good Lord! how she laughed! and begging me to get up and not make such a fool of myself."

"And did not that cure you?" in a breath-less tone.

"Cure me! bless your heart, no! I went on sobbing; you might have heard me from Thames to Tweed. Mine was no silent afflic-tion, I can assure you."

Joan's eyes are fastened upon the broad sheet of big yellow St. John's worts that help to floor bravely the wood. They are nearly over now; here and there is a broad disk, with its crowded stamens, to which Time delays saying, "Pass! begone!" Until to-day she has always thought them handsome joyous-featured flowers.

"On my knees," repeats Anthony with a healthy heart-whole smile, "as if any woman were ever won by such an attitude! Next time I will go on all-fours."

"Did you know that she was coming to-day?" asks the girl, absently picking a straw-berry-leaf, and closely looking with unseeing eyes at its notched edge.

"Until two days ago I had not an idea of it. It is a kind surprise that my mother has contrived for me." Silence—perfect silence—warm, sleepy, fir-scented. "I was certainly very bad," says Anthony presently, with the sane and wholesome smile of complete recovery still lighting up his face. "I sank so low that I kissed her door-knocker— a grimy London door-knocker. Figure to yourself that! I kissed the area railings; I think I kissed the butcher's boy."

"And now," says Joan, gallantly striving to speak in a tone of gay and indifferent friendliness as one that relishes a good jest, and to keep wholly out of her face and voice

the dull flat pain that has taken its seat at
her heart. "And now I suppose that it will
all have to be done over again. At 5.50"
(with a strained smile) "your agony will re-
commence."

"Will it?" cries the young man ex-
pressively; "on the contrary, I live in hopes
of seeing a successor or two vivisected. I
have invited a couple of men with an express
view to that object. No! no!" shaking his
head with a cheerful gravity, "she will not
try that again."

"But if she does try?" asks Joan in a low
quick voice, turning away her face so that he
may not see the unseemly greedy eagerness
for his answer written on every one of its
poor features.

"Let her!" says Anthony valiantly. "I
defy her! look at me—look at me straight!
I do not believe that in your life you have
ever looked full at me! There, that is
better!" as under the compulsion of his voice

she meekly lifts her eyes to his, and in those great pupils he sees himself

"Mirrored small in Paradise."

"Let her do her worst—her very worst, and that is pretty bad, I can tell you. No" (with a sudden change of tone), "I will not say that, either; it is bad luck to boast; 'he that thinketh he standeth let him take heed lest he fall.' I am sure that I ought not to fall, for I never think that I stand."

She has dropped her eyes again in irresistible dejection. They have failed to catch any of the confidence of his.

"But without brag," continues the young man in a brave and joyous tone, "I think I may safely say that if, in the course of the next fortnight, I walk round the room on my knees after any woman, it will not be after her!"

A couple of hours later they are both standing before the closed door of the morning-room, listening.

"Would it be dishonourable to apply one's

eye to the keyhole?" asks Anthony in a tone half humorous, half grave. After a moment: "No, it is not necessary, she has come; I hear her voice. Last time that I heard it I was staggering about as if I were drunk !— do I stagger now? Your necktie is not so white as I was !—am I white now? My pulse was tearing along at a gallop—it hardly trots now; will you feel it?" She shakes her head with a little gesture of refusal. " I will have a bet with you," says the young man in an eager whisper, " that at the present moment yours is beating more quickly than mine !" As he speaks he takes hold of her small wrist and lays his fingers upon it. " What a weak little quick tick-tack !" he says tenderly; then, suddenly stooping his comely head, he softly and hurriedly kisses one of the little blue veins that, like fine threads, wander beneath the cream of her fair skin. " There !" he says, " I am bucklered and panoplied ! Let us go in."

CHAPTER XXI.

"A whitely wanton with a velvet brow."

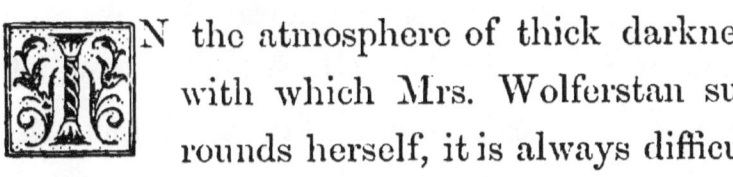N the atmosphere of thick darkness with which Mrs. Wolferstan surrounds herself, it is always difficult —more especially to one coming in straight from the universal glare of day—to distinguish one thing or person from another. In Mrs. Wolferstan's shrine a young man may always be mistaken for an old woman, a dog for a cat, and *vice versa*. It is, therefore, not quite instantaneously that Joan makes out which of the two sitting figures is the new arrival. A moment, however, decides it. It must be the stranger who, at their entry, rises with

supple-jointed briskness, and comes to meet them, stretching out her hands and crying in a tone of joy and relief :

" Ah ! you are here at last ; but you have been as long in coming as the millennium. How are you, Anthony ? What a long time it is since we have met !—four ?—five years ? it seems like a hundred !"

" Perhaps it is," answers Anthony, readily taking in his both the offered hands, and speaking in a tone and with a laugh in which even Joan's jealous ears fail to detect the smallest grain of fevered unreality or effort. " If it is we have both worn pretty well, have not we ?"

" It is impossible here to see how we have worn !" answers the girl, glancing round discontentedly at the tinted dusk. " Mrs. Wolferstan, I may pull up one of the blinds, may not I ? Why do you keep the room so dark—are your eyes weak ?"

Without waiting for answer or permission, she touches the blind-cord, and up springs the

red blind and in flows the golden afternoon
light, that has been only waiting outside
for the smallest encouragement to pour in its
liberal flood.

"Ah, that is better!" cries Lalage cheerfully. She has taken her ex-lover familiarly
by the hand, and has led him into the deep
bow of the window, where she is now coolly
and boldly scanning his features at her leisure. "I see no crowsfeet!" she says, with
a light laugh; "do you? Yes, we have worn
pretty well:

"'Time writes no wrinkles on our azure brows.'"

For the first few seconds after the upward
rush of the blind, an irresistible feeling of
fear and repugnance has hindered Joan from
looking at her rival. Now an equally uncon-
querable instinct of curiosity turns her eyes
towards the woman for whose fair sake
Anthony thought it worth while painfully to
travel round the room on his knees, and tear-
fully to kiss an unresponsive door-knocker.

The first glance reveals that she is plump.

She has taken that earliest step towards a man's esteem and affection. She looks again. Eyes moderate in size, narrow in shape, but brimful of a cold quick devilry, sparkling like icicles on a winter's day; a short and rather paltry nose; a skin that by-and-by will be streaky and raddled, but where now carnations lose themselves in milk; a merry, bold, red mouth; a face that if you take away its colouring is nothing, that if you look at it in profile is nothing, that if you pick it to pieces is nothing, but which, through sheer gaudiness of hue and splendour of animal life, drives you into hotter commendation than you often give to more real loveliness.

Joan looks away again, utterly unadmiring herself, but with a chill misgiving that her want of appreciation is unlikely to be shared by anything male; flesh and colour—good of their kind and plenty of them—being generally all that is needed to snare the eyes and evoke the encomiums of any member of that simple race. She looks away just in time to catch a glimpse of Mrs. Wolferstan's white muslin tail vanishing through the door.

"Why has Mrs. Wolferstan disappeared?" asks Lalage, releasing the young man from her scrutiny and advancing again into the room. "Because I pulled up the blind?— not really?—why, we were all *groping!*"

"She dislikes a strong light," says Anthony apologetically, stepping out of the window as he speaks, and lighting a cigar as an excuse for not re-entering.

"Rather hard that a whole household should be sacrificed on the altar of one complexion, is not it?" cries Lalage as soon as he is out of earshot. "I have no notion of such selfishness. I shall make a point of keeping that blind—yes, and one of the others too—up during the whole of my stay!"

Joan laughs a little disbelievingly. "Will you?"

"Do you suppose that you and I comprise the whole party?" asks Lalage, lowering her voice a little, and stepping confidentially nearer. "Heaven forbid! There must be some one else coming—some men. I hate a petticoat party, do not you?" Without waiting for an answer she goes on : " I always think it argues such conceit in people asking you to meet just themselves—just a family party. I abhor a family party!"

A little silence. To Joan, the problem of the door-knocker is becoming more and more insoluble. In ten years how coarse she will be—she will have three chins! They are already faintly foreshadowed. What a strong-armed lady's-maid—what mighty holdings of the breath must have gone to the making of that nipped-in waist!

" It seems a capital house!" says Lalage presently, casting a quick and appraising eye round ; " are all the reception-rooms as good as this? Better?—bravo! I had no idea that it was this stamp of place at all; Anthony never gave me a hint of it."

Joan smiles sardonically.

" Ah! there is Anthony again!" cries the

other, walking quickly back to the window, and beginning to nod her head and smile; " he pretends that he does not see me, but I know better. Dear old Tony! how well he looks! he has filled out since the days I used to know him; those big-boned gawky boys make the best men after all, do not they?"

" Yes."

" I suppose that no one but me calls him Tony?" says the girl, turning her head over her shoulder to ask the question; " no?—I thought not! Tony Lumpkin I used to call him! How angry it made him! ha! ha!"

    *   *   *   *   *

Though it would not seem that such a toilette as Joan's—dead black gown, and live white roses—would take a very long time in making, yet she is quite the last of the guests to make her appearance; entering, indeed, at the same moment as the butler, who announces dinner. It is therefore not till all are seated, drawing off gloves, and making the vital decision between Julienne and Bisque, that she

is able to master the details of the party.
How different the table looks! so greatly
elongated! and how far off Anthony! Old
Mr. Wolferstan, his wheeled chair and his
austere valet, have disappeared; relegated to
an upper chamber. She turns her eyes slowly
round the table, examining each face in turn.
How familiar they all are, or rather used to
be to her! How constantly at ball and drum
and dinner has she nightly met them! It
seems like coming back from the dead to be
amongst them again. She always used to
keep half a dozen round dances at every ball
for that big guardsman opposite. He and
Anthony were her two favourite partners.
She never could quite make up her mind
which of the two she liked best. Is that
possible?

With a feeling of incredulity, she involuntarily glances again at distant Anthony. He
is saying some little gay civil thing to the
old woman on his right hand — a real old
woman, who does not disdain to be an old

woman, but wears a real cap with strings; and of her elderly charms, judiciously exhibits nothing but face and hands. Finding out by the magnetism which always tells a person, when they are steadily regarded, that his love's fair eyes are upon him, he breaks off in the middle of a sentence to turn his head, and send her down the long table a smile—small enough to travel unnoticed past the intervening guests—large enough to warm her chilly heart. She looks quickly back again at the grenadier. Is it possible? And if the cases had been reversed, if chance had established her aunt and cousins, and consequently herself, at the big guardsman's gates, instead of at Anthony's, would she have loved him instead? Is it such a mere matter of accident?

"Must I always love the man who is nearest to me?" she asks herself, with a feeling of shocked self-contempt: a moment's reflection, however, reinstates her in her self-esteem. "No! Micky is far the nearest to me, and I am certainly at some distance from loving him!"

She is so busy with her thoughts that people are half way through their fish before she recollects how entirely she is neglecting her own escort. He is a little attaché whom she used to snub. Dear me! how many years it seems since she has had the heart to snub any one! With hasty penitence, recollecting herself, she makes some slight observation to him, but has no sooner uttered it than she perceives that her remorse has been wasted. He does not even hear her. Between every two mouthfuls he is sending glances, heavy-laden with silent approbation, across the table to Lalage, who, more than ever looking as if she were made out of roses and cream—a great many roses, and a great deal of cream—nearly faces him. To do her justice, she is for the moment not thinking of him. She is eating pink salmon, and pondering, with her eyes on the menu, as to which entrées she will choose, and whether she will be able to enjoy three of them, or had better content herself with two.

People are seldom rightly sorted on the first day of a party. They are like odd gloves promiscuously coupled together; two left-hand ones, two right-hand ones.

In the present instance, had they been left to themselves, the guardsman would have chosen Joan and the attaché Lalage; whereas now the guardsman has Lalage and the attaché Joan. The attaché does not care for Joan, and the guardsman does not like Lalage. When the end of dinner frees them from their enforced bonds, the true bent of their dispositions will be seen. Soon seen now; for the ladies have been ten minutes in the drawing-room, and thank God the days of long post-cœnal drinking are over and gone.

Five minutes more will probably bring them; but for the moment they are not come. There is no sound to be heard but the low hum of women's voices, the thin dry croak of the old ones, and the round liquid

babble of the young. Of the latter indeed,
two are contributing nothing to the conversation.   One is asleep, and the other, though
wideawake, is dumb.

The sleeping one is Lalage.   Immediately
on coming into the drawing-room she has
thrown herself into the most comfortable
chair in the room—a chair exclusively conse-
crated to Mrs. Wolferstan's use, and in which
it is a point of honour that no one else shall
ever sit.   It is a long low fauteuil of peculiar
construction, and its position, by a careful
arrangement of shaded light above and around
it, combines in the highest possible degree the
becoming and the luxurious.

" I am afraid that I have taken your chair,
have not I ?" says Lalage in a drowsy voice,
without offering to move, as she sees Mrs.
Wolferstan hover about with wistful and
meaning looks, like a bird round its robbed
nest ; " I am so sorry ! you do not mind ?
no ?—well then I will not make you uncomfortable by moving ; it is certainly very

well stuffed; please wake me if I fall asleep!"

"I am glad that you like it!" says the other, with a stunted smile; "it was quite my own idea! I took a good deal of pains about it; Howard himself took my directions, but" (with a little dry laugh) "we all know that my tastes are in many ways rather peculiar; most people—and I fancy you—would prefer one of these others!"

"Thank you, no!" replies Lalage, closing her eyes, and speaking in a voice on which coming slumber is already beginning to tell; "this exactly fits the nape of my neck!"

There is no more to be said, and Mrs. Wolferstan retires discomfited, only to fall into the clutches of the old lady whom Anthony took in to dinner; who, for the punishment of her sins, happens to have been at school with her, and now proceeds to burn her on a slow fire of reminiscences and dates. Joan has placed herself in a little nooky recess by an open window, her body almost hidden by the low droop of an ample curtain, and her cheek swept by the softness of the night wind. It is so soft, it feels like feathers blowing against her face.

"I will not challenge his notice!" she says to herself with a resolute pride; "I will not be on the lookout for him; if he find me, it shall be because he comes to seek me!"

As the thought passes through her brain the door opens and the men begin to enter. At the first click of the door-handle Lalage wakes, with no start or suddenness, but with a little rosy stretch and yawn, like a drowsy child. They must all pass by her luxurious lair; she can therefore conveniently pounce upon whichever of them she wishes to engage in conversation. One, two, three pass by unmolested. Not a word or a look detains them. The fourth is Anthony. Will he also escape? It will not be his fault if he does not. There is no purpose of halting in his face: his quick eyes look ahead of him as one that seeks but has not yet found. But

Lalage is not to be balked by any such small impediment. As he passes within a foot of her, she raises herself from her reclining posture ; and stretching out one large white arm, lightly touches him on the coat-sleeve with her fan, looking up in his face the while. She has shaken the sleep from her eyes ; nor do they any longer seem to be wanting in either size or sweetness. At the same moment she speaks. Joan is too far off to be able to catch her words ; but, by her look, she judges that they are both kind and salted. Perforce he stops. At the same instant Joan grows aware that her own retreat has become a *solitude à deux,* and that a hearty man's voice is saying to her :

"Where have you been hiding yourself all this year ?"

She starts a little, and perceives that the faithful guardsman's body has at length been able to follow whither, all through dinner, heart and eyes had led him, and is now deposited in solid comeliness beside her, with every apparent intention of making a considerable stay.

" Have I hidden myself?"

" I did not meet you once in London this season !"

" I was not to be met."

" Have you already given up the world ?" (laughing).

" It has given me up !" she answers gravely.

As she speaks her eyes again stray furtively away. Lalage is wideawake now; leaning well forward with arms crossed on her lap. She is the only *décolleté* woman in the room ; but then, probably, no other woman in the room has such a bust to exhibit. If they had they would possibly be no more backward in advertising it than she. What a neck it is ! What a great deal of it ! What a smooth sea of pearl ! What shoulders ! What arms ! absolutely unclothed but for the two tiny shoulder-straps, which alone hinder her garment from entirely taking French leave. With a sickening heart Joan takes in these luxurious details.

"There is hope as long as he does not sit down!" she says to herself; "as long as he stands—as long as he stands!"

As she so thinks, there comes a lull in the universal buzz of talk—one of those curious gaps when everybody's ideas seem to fail them at the same moment. Lalage only still speaks, and Joan's sharpened ears have no difficulty in catching her utterance.

"Would you mind deciding whether you mean to go or stay? to sit down or to walk away? I should be glad if you would do either the one or the other!" By the gesture with which she accompanies this remark—a gesture which points confidently to a neighbouring chair, it is evident which alternative she expects him to choose. But for once she reckons without her host.

"I will do the other," he answers, lightly laughing, and moving off with a haste somewhat suggestive of a fear of being recalled.

But Lalage does not recall him. She only looks after him for a moment, without anger, but with a little surprised shrugging of shoulder and raising of brows; then, resettling herself among her cushions, turns, with a contented if sleepy smile, to the attaché, who has pounced like a hungry hawk upon Anthony's neglected opportunity.

"You are wise," she says with lazy approbation; "you sit down. I cannot understand any one standing when they can sit, or waking when they can sleep. Can you?" To herself she says, "I shall have more difficulty than I thought in warming up the old broth!"

Meanwhile the chair on Joan's other hand has become occupied, and in consequence it seems to her eyes as if in this dim recess a hundred candles had been suddenly lit.

"A rose between two thorns!" she says gaily, smiling first upon one, then on the other; though, did he but know it, the guardsman's smile is of a poorer quality than the other.

"Do not you think that one thorn at a time is enough for any rose?" asks Anthony, looking across at his fellow-soldier, and emphasising this broad hint by the urgency of his eyes. He has done his brother-in-arms many a good turn in his day, in the way of backing him up when needed, and effacing himself when not needed; and he thinks the present a good opportunity for exacting a return in kind.

The grenadier looks at Joan. It seems to him, *à priori*, a little unlikely, that any woman should wish to be rid of him; but in her eyes, gentle and playful as they are, he can read no slightest desire to detain him. He therefore bows to destiny and goes.

The two friends remain alone behind the curtain. Half an hour later a French window is stealthily opened. Wolferstan is already standing outside on the terrace. Joan hovers undecided on the sill.

"You may set your prudish soul at rest,"

he is saying a little impatiently; "some one has already broken the ice. See that white gown among the trees! whose is it? which of you wears a white gown?"

Joan looks back over her shoulder into the lit room to see who is missing.

" It is Miss Beauchamp!"

He gives a slight start, then laughs.

"Of course! what a fool I was to ask!"

Without more speech on either side she joins him, and they begin to walk a little, to Joan's surprise, in the direction of the white gown. It is Lalage!— Lalage—on a garden-seat, surrounded by all her little comforts: an escort to keep the gnats away; a little pillow to protect her soft shoulders from the cold iron of the chair-back; a footstool to lift her feet out of the dews.

" Your mother keeps her rooms too hot!" she says, raising friendly starlit eyes to Anthony. "Why do not you tell her? I shall speak to her about it myself to-mor-

row; old people have no blood in their veins,
I suppose. I was asphyxiated—feel how I
burn !"

As she speaks she stretches out her hand
to him, and he must needs take it. Joan
looks away, conscientiously trying not to observe how long he holds that substantial snow-
flake. She is recalled by Lalage's voice, lazy
and bland.

"Do you want to sit down? No? That
is right ! there is room for two here, but there
is not room for four."

"A hint for us to make ourselves scarce !"
says Anthony, laughing ; and they move away.
For some paces they do not speak. Then :

"And I walked round the room on my
knees after her !" says Wolferstan, tragi-
comically.

"Yes."

"To her mind's eye I am always on my
knees. I suppose," he goes on dryly, "she
never sees me in any other posture. I must
ask her if it is so !"

" Yes ?"

It is a little light word, but to her in the uttering it seems long and leaden-weighted.

" I do not mean *now!*" says the young man rather hastily ; " not yet awhile, but by-and-by—by-and-by—when — when circumstances have proved to her that I can have no desire to repeat the operation."

CHAPTER XXII.

THE night is gone, and another day is come, young, clear, and shining; a bran new coin fresh from God's mint. There are only six now left to Joan of her visit—only six—and then the deluge; worse than the deluge, indeed, for the deluge was at least a cleanly phenomenon, and Portland Villa is not. Six days! and then the wrecked crockery, the lumpy bed, the affluent dirt, the greasy victual, Bell, Micky! She runs up the scale of her afflictions, and high, high up above all the others sits Mr. Brand in his red tunic.

Of this day, however, not very much has as yet gone—not more than half the morning at least. Breakfast has been over some little time; breakfast—no longer the cosy duet when He and She wooed each other with tea and marmalade. To-day he is almost out of sight, and quite out of speech. However, things might be worse, for he has an old woman on his right hand, and a man on his left, and Lalage does not appear. She prefers the privacy of a heavy-laden tray in her bedroom.

It is midday and past when Joan, entering the morning room, finds her at length descended and engaged in colloquy with her hostess, who has made a heroic effort over herself, and faced the staring morning sun a good hour earlier than is her wont. It is only for the fag end of the conversation that Joan comes in. Two of the blinds are drawn up, and Mrs. Wolferstan is sitting in a corner with a hat on and a veil down. She has not been out of doors, and is not going.

"There exists no greater advocate for early marriages than I," she is saying in her high frosty voice; "I mean for men; it keeps them out of—well, we do not know what it does not keep them out of!—it is what I am always preaching to Anthony. He knows my way so well now, that as soon as I begin the subject he—flies! Well," with a sigh, "I suppose that his hour has not yet come."

"I suppose not," answers Lalage, with a curious smile, as she stands basking in the full stream of the sunlight; "how old were you when you married?"

"I, my dear! do not ask me!" raising her pale hands with a chilly laugh; "I was a baby—an infant. You would not believe me if I were to tell you how absurdly innocent I was the first time that Mr. Wolferstan saw me. I was in short frocks! positively I was playing with my doll! and yet, curious, is not it? he has often and often told me since that the first moment he saw me he said to himself, 'That is my wife.'"

"And sure enough, so it was!" says Lalage, still smiling, and gently rubbing with one little shoe the back, half-shorn, half-curly, of a poodle dog, who is taking a sun bath at her feet. "What an odd sensation it would be to see a strange man come into the room, and say to oneself, 'That is my husband!' I cannot say that I ever had occasion to make the remark; had you, Miss Dering?"

Joan shakes her brown head and laughs.

"Never! I should be too much afraid of his contradicting me and saying, 'No, it is not!'"

"It is not fair to ask you these delicate questions in public, is it?" rejoins the other with a laugh. "Come out on the terrace, and confide in me." As she speaks she puts her hand through Joan's slight arm, and draws her away through the French window, and into the outside air and sun-blaze beyond. As soon as they are out of earshot: "Was not that well done ?" she cries triumphantly ; "but for my presence of mind we should have remained roasting on the spit of her remi- niscences till luncheon-time. After all, there is nothing like presence of mind."

Joan smiles a little ironically.

" Nothing !"

" If I had stayed five minutes longer I should have had to have asked her to let me take her to pieces," says Lalage, lower- ing her voice to a confidential tone. " I long to see how much of her stays on ; do not you know ?—and how much comes off ! My ima- gination always will take these odious flights ; I wish it did not. I never see a preposte- rously fat person that I do not instantly picture them in their bath !"

Joan smiles, and stoops to pat Anthony's colly, which galloped up, young, rude and well-meaning a moment ago.

" She is not a nice old woman !" continues Lalage, curling up her white nose in dis- pleased recollection of her hostess; " far

from it! but even if she were, I should not
like her: I dislike all old people!"

"*All?*"

"Yes, all!—now I come to think of it, it
is only a very small proportion of the human
race that I find agreeable; as I tell you, I
have a distaste for old people. No one can
really like children, though few have the
moral courage to own it; the lower orders are
in every respect offensive; and between ourselves—of course I do not give this out generally—this is quite in your ear—but between
you and me, I am not very fond of the sick
and afflicted."

"If I fall ill then I will not ask you to
nurse me;" says Joan, with a grave smile,
gently pulling the dog's ear, as he walks, hot
and friendly, beside her.

"No, do not!" answers Lalage, seriously.
"I should be so sorry to refuse, but, if you
understand, when any one is ill or in trouble,
my impulse always is to go away—I dislike
seeing it!" A moment later: "The other

day I heard of a very religious woman who said that she never saw a cripple without longing to throw a stone at him. Do you comprehend what she meant? No? Well I do!"

They have left the well-rolled gravel terrace, a simultaneous impulse prompts them to seek a tree's shelter for their uncovered heads. Across the scorched grass, which smells like ready-made hay, they go slowly trailing; a fair white woman, a fair black woman, side by side. Presently—

"How long have you been here?" asks Lalage abruptly.

"A week—a week yesterday."

"By yourself the whole time? No other visitor?"

"No other."

"A whole week of undiluted Mrs. Wolferstan?" cries Lalage, raising her eyebrows and spreading out her prosperous white hands, "Are you sure that you are really quite alive? But ah!" (correcting herself, and with a meaning look,) "of course there were alleviating circumstances !"

Joan looks straight ahead of her, and tries to believe that the flush which she is aware is very considerable when seen in full face, may be hardly perceptible in profile. They have reached the shady domain of a great beech tree. Under his protection they sit down and pant.

" In a week," says Lalage reflectively, "you must have gone pretty well through her autobiography ; you have heard, no doubt, of the time when she could compass her own waist with her finger and thumb ?"

Joan smiles reluctantly, " Yes."

" And of the bootmaker who borrowed her old shoe to exhibit in a glass case in his shop window ?"

" Yes."

" And of the clergyman who fell down in a fit and foamed at the mouth in the middle of the Litany, because she came into church in a chip hat ?"

Joan shakes her head. " No."

" And of—"

But Joan interrupts her. " Stay !" she says, laying her gentle hand on the other's lawny sleeve. " You make me laugh against my will ; it is dishonest to eat a person's bread, and then ridicule them !"

" Pooh !" cries Lalage airily, " it is not her bread—it is Anthony's ; at least that is the way I always look at it. Whose ever it is, it is very good bread ; I never wish to eat better marrow patties than those were last night," she adds thoughtfully. A moment later, looking up discontentedly at the not quite impervious bough-roof above her head, " How much one feels the sun, even here. What a misfortune a thin skin is ! I shall be as freckled as a turkey's egg—you cannot conceive how I freckle !"

" Do you ?"

" Oh, if some good Samaritan would but fetch me a parasol—an umbrella—anything— from the house ! Oh, Miss Dering," (in a wheedling tone,) " if you would but run across the grass—it is not more than a hundred yards—and fetch me one. Your legs are longer than mine—I will do as much for you when I am as slight as you are."

" I will go with pleasure," says Joan, rising with good-natured alacrity; " where shall I find it ?"

" In the hall—in my room—anywhere," replies Lalage vaguely. " But you do not mean to say that you are going really ? Yes ? That is right. And while you are about it you may as well bring me a hat too—the one with the brigade ribbon—oh ! and gloves—a *peau de Suède* pair," (stroking the satiny back of her own hand). " There could not be a deeper depth of degradation than freckled hands, could there ?"

Joan is away ten good minutes. Firstly, Miss Beauchamp's maid is not forthcoming, then the hat with the brigade ribbon has mislaid itself; then she forgets the *peau de Suède* gloves, and has to go back for them;

but at length, obediently laden with all that she has been bidden to fetch, she returns to the beech-tree seat.

It is empty—Lalage has disappeared. Not quite disappeared either; for, as she casts her eyes round the landscape, Joan sees her late companion slowly vanishing down one of the garden alleys in the direction of the wood. By her side is a male form which she has no difficulty in recognising. Indeed, when one is interested in a person, it is singular by how small and distant a portion of him one can swear to his identity. She sits down on the deserted seat and leans her hot face against the cool and smooth beech-bark.

" It is beginning !" she says to herself, " it is beginning !"

She has come hurriedly, and the sun was strong and cruel. She puts up her hand to her head, then passes her fingers over her eyes, which have suddenly grown misty. They are on the edge of the wood-skirts now. In a moment they will have plunged into it, and be lost to sight. But how is this? They have stopped. For a moment they speak together, then the man looks back; not only looks back but turns back. Not content with quickly walking, he is running over the grass towards her. In a few moments he is beside her.

"You have come to fetch these?" she says, holding up the hat and gloves in one hand and the parasol in the other, and lifting patient eyes, quite dry now, to his face. "I am sorry that I was so slow, but two or three things hindered me! will you tell her?"

"Tell whom?" asks Anthony, eyeing the properties offered to his notice with a somewhat puzzled air; "oh! I see!" (a light dawning on his intelligence and flashing in a rather angry smile over his face); "she has been making you her errand boy! how like her!"

"Her errand girl, you mean!" says Joan, with a little laugh and shrug; "I did not mind! what does it matter? it is all in the day's work!"

"It is not in *your* day's work!" returns Wolferstan, trenchantly; "I will not have you made anybody's errand boy, or errand girl either! if you run on any more errands you and I shall quarrel, do you hear?"

There is such a tone of authority and appropriation in his voice that her heart gives one great joy leap, but she answers coolly and lightly:

"I fear then that our peace will be of short duration, for I foresee that before ten minutes are over she will send me in again for a neckerchief, or a foot-stool, or a book; and I am so weak-minded that I shall certainly go! by-the-bye, had not you better take these to her at once" (making a fresh tender of hat, gloves, and sunshade), "she is waiting!"

"Let her wait!" replies Wolferstan gruffly.

He has sat down; and, having plucked a low drooping little beech-bough, is fanning the flushed bronze of his face with it.

"You did not come on purpose to fetch them then?" says Joan, with an unavoidable streak of satisfaction in her voice, as she idly thrusts her fingers into Lalage's too roomy gloves.

"To fetch these!—certainly not! I came to fetch you!"

"To fetch me?"

"Yes, you."

"What!" she says, colouring slightly, "have you never heard that 'two is company and three is trumpery'?"

He laughs.

"In this case the sentiment is as false as the rhyme; in this case 'three is company and two is trumpery'!"

She looks at him with a small fine smile.

"Are you afraid of a relapse? do you want me to take care of you?"

He is resting his sunshiny head against the beech trunk, close to hers. Not three inches of beech bark intervene between the tips of their two noses.

"That is exactly what I do want!" he answers gravely; and for once his eyes confirm the utterance of his lips; "you have taken the words out of my mouth; but I am not at all afraid of a relapse, thank you!"

CHAPTER XXIII.

HE days darken into nights: the nights slide into days; and now the second week of Joan's visit has gone to join the first. To-morrow, the party is to break up; and every one to go their different way. The hungry past, who is not satisfied with less than everything, whose ever-famished mouth gapes for all our paltry minutes, has swallowed it too. It has not gone quite so quickly as its fore-runner perhaps. It has been fuller of little incidents. In it, there has been less of sweet swift monotony. Fourteen days! Each

night, when she went to bed, has Joan
grudgingly deducted one from the poor little
sum, and now she has come to the fourteenth
and last.   In this case, the last has certainly
not been the best.   It has been a day devoted
to an expedition, which, like nineteen out of
every twenty enforced pleasure-parties, has
turned out a failure.   The weather has been
disagreeable : the luncheon went astray :
everybody has been mismated.   Those who
have had no desire for each other's proximity
have, during a twelve mile drive, been packed,
side by side, and knee to knee, in barouche
and waggonette.   Those who have yearned
for each other's society, have seen themselves,
hopelessly parted, in separate vehicles.   But
this abortive fête is dead and over now, so
one may forgive it.   Everybody is dressed,
and hungrily looking dinnerwards.

"For whom are we waiting ?" Lalage asks,
in an impatient voice, of Joan, by whom she
has seated herself; "it is five minutes past
eight! mostly they are punctual : I hate

being kept waiting for my dinner, do not you? it takes the edge off one's appetite! Good Heavens!"—in an altered tone—"'Who are these like stars appearing?' has dear old Jezebel hired a company of mountebanks for the evening?"

Joan looks up just in time to see the butler throw wide the high-folding doors, and hear him announce with equal gravity and distinctness, "Mrs. and the Misses Moberley!" She gives a great start, and rubs her eyes. Is it a very odious dream? Not so, Joan! It is a cheek-reddening, heart-sinking, pride-basing reality.

Mrs. Moberley, leading the van and filling the doorway; Mrs. Moberley in cotton-backed satin with gaping placket hole, and straining seams: on her breast a vast landscape brooch, comprising a castellated residence and three forest trees in bog oak. On her head, a large wild cap, once, no doubt, a princely coiffure, but now, through time and ill-usage, reduced to being, like the Coliseum, a superb wreck.

Behind her step her two fair daughters, clad in draggling muslin gowns of the strongest possible pink; fans tightly grasped, held upright like sceptres, in their hands; and towering heads that smite the sky, and where all the fowls of the air might roost.

It is clear, indeed, that Diana has reft Micky's bird of paradise plume from her hat, and stuck it into her hair, where, in company with a high comb, a nation of beads, and a large bunch of roses, it now waves in sociable triumph. It is no dream. Before they are well in the room, she hears Bell's mighty voice, thrusting itself forward before mother and sister, in exaggerated apology for their lateness. Joan is roused from her painful surprise by a low laugh of zest and merriment from Lalage.

" I do not know which I like best," she is saying in a choked voice; " the old lady with the timber ornaments is very nice, but I think on the whole, I give the prize to the young woman with the voice and the cheeks, who looks as if she were sitting for a picture of Eolus!—why do not you laugh?—do not they amuse you?"

"They are my aunt and cousins—my first cousins!—I live with them," replies Joan, whitening a good deal, and speaking with a great effort, but quite quietly and distinctly.

"What!" cries the other, glancing hastily at her face, to see whether she is serious, and looking a little out of countenance—" not really?—are you quite sure? how very un- fortunate! but it is no use my eating my words, is it?—what is said is said!—I can but request the earth to open and swallow me up!"

At the same moment, Joan is aware that her hostess is approaching, with her usual undulating girl-gait, and with several slips of folded paper in her hand.

"We are going to make a little change to-night," she says with her frozen suavity, "do you mind?—we have no great sticklers for precedence among us, and it is tiresome always to go in to dinner in the same order, is not it?—so to-night the ladies are to draw lots for the gentlemen; will you draw?—it makes a change!" and so passes on to deliver her little address to the next person.

Joan has obeyed; and now, having peeped with trembling quickness at the fateful morsel, crumples it up in her hand. "Wrong! wrong! everything is going wrong to-day, and it is the last day!"

All the ladies are now provided with their slips of paper, and are mastering their contents. Lalage is opening hers with leisurely indifference.

" Heaven send me some one who will let me eat my dinner in peace!" she says; a moment later having learnt her fate, she holds out the paper with a half mischievous smile to Joan, crying, " Shall we change?"

Mrs. Moberley is fumbling for her spectacles, and, missing her pocket, gropes in her placket hole till dinner. Bell, with craned neck, is sending her dauntless eye round the

room in excited enquiry, as to which of all
the equally unknown men, owns the name
she has drawn. Diana is flushing uncom-
fortably, and looking shy. Dinner is an-
nounced; and, reversing the usual order of
things, there is a stir among the ladies, and
the men stand still. Joan rises and crosses
the room with a lagging step—he is a long
way off—to her guardsman.

"I believe that you are my fate!" she says
with a not very elated smile; nor does she
even hear his expressions of pleasure at his
good luck, for her thoughts have travelled
away with her eyes, and are following Lalage, as she gaily and briskly walks up to
Wolferstan; and putting her hand through
his arm, as she looks up in his face with a
familiar smile, cries : " Here I am ! pray try
to look a little pleased."

Bell, having at length mastered his identity,
has pounced upon the ill-fated attaché, and
proudly sailed out with him before half the
dowagers.

Mrs. Moberley, still searching for her spectacles, remains seated on her sofa, in hopeless perplexity, until compassionately picked up by a surplus man.

And now the newly-assorted assembly are all seated; and, however ill-paired, have to make the best of each other for the next hour and a half. It is always a rash thing to say that any one portion of one's existence is distinctly the most disagreeable that one has ever spent; but in after-times Joan was wont to think that—(setting aside the great griefs of her life)—there were few portions of her history that she would less soon have over again than that one dinner and August evening.

There is hardly one of the table dispositions with which she is not inclined to quarrel. The person whom she would fain be near is farther from her than any one else. At his right hand, tantalizingly out of earshot, but well in sight, sits Lalage, her head wreathed with real vine-leaves, like a Bacchante ; Lalage, with fewer clothes and more neck than ever ; Lalage making jokes she cannot hear, and shooting eye-shafts that she cannot hinder. Exactly opposite her sits Bell. Within one of Bell, Mrs. Moberley ; within one of Mrs. Moberley, Diana. Thus all her relations face her ; nor is she spared one humiliating detail of their conduct and appearance. She is recalled from her mortifying reflections by the voice of her neighbour.

"Do tell me about these natives ! where on earth did Mrs. Wolferstan pick them up ? Did you ever see a more appalling spectacle than the one with the big face—our *vis-à-vis*, I mean ? she is out-and-out the worst !"

"They are my aunt and cousins," says Joan, in an extinguished voice, writhing a little. "I live with them."

The young man breaks into a delighted laugh ; he thinks it a joke.

"Your aunt and cousins ! what a capital idea ! had not you better say your mother and sisters at once ?"

" But they are," cries poor Joan, in an agony, turning first a painful scarlet, then as white as the table-cloth; "they are my aunt and cousins—my first cousins—and I live with them! Oh, please understand that I am quite serious! please" (looking round the table miserably), "please let every one know that they are my relations."

Something in the irritated anguish of her tone at length convinces her partner of his error.

" Good God!" he cries, his mirth suddenly quenched, "how very awful!—I—I—had not an idea—I—really—I do not know what to say—I—I—thought you were joking."

" I know you did," says Joan, gasping a little, and stretching out her hand towards a water-bottle; "but do not ever think so again. I never joke."

They subside into an uncomfortable silence. Joan looks round the table again. When first they had sat down, Anthony had sent her from his distant place a look full of discontent and discomfiture at their separation; gathered brows and downward-curving lips plainly expressing his displeasure. She glances at him now. His forehead is quite smooth, and the corners of his mouth are curling jovially upwards again, according to their merry wont. Lalage is leaning her vine-bound head towards him, and is apparently telling him some anecdote at which he is laughing immoderately. Probably it is a highly-spiced one, for it is only a strongly-seasoned jest that ever moves a man to such extravagance of mirth. It is of course right and fit that the host should look amiably at, and talk merrily to, such of his guests as neighbour him; but Joan wishes that he did not do it quite so well.

As for Lalage, she looks to-night as if— were she in her right place—she would be dancing and cymballing, and tossing white arms with fauns and hoofed satyrs, and tipsy wood-gods, down a green forest-glade.

Joan turns her eyes away, and perforce they fall upon her *vis-à-vis*. The attaché,

through soup and fish-time, has exhibited
his distaste for his situation by a sulky silence.
He now changes his tactics, and begins to dis-
play his ill-humour by indulging in the kindly
pastime of drawing out Miss Moberley; an
exercise than which he never in his life set
himself one easier of accomplishment. Joan
would give anything she possesses to be
able not to see how fearfully well he succeeds,
would readily sacrifice a year of life to be able
not to hear her cousin's observations. But it
is impossible to put one's fingers in one's ears
in a mixed company; and nothing short of
that could keep out the sound of Bell's
powerful voice, which, as the dinner pro-
gresses, grows ever more triumphantly loud.
Her giggling waxes more incessant; from her
hair, loosened by the continual playful tossings
and shakings of her head, the hair-pins begin
to drop; excitement, pride and heat cause the
profound red of her cheeks to overflow her
forehead, and invade her neck.

At last, when Joan has begun to cast over

seriously in her mind whether she cannot
feign a nose-bleeding or a swoon, to deliver
her from a situation of such wretchedness,
Mrs. Wolferstan puts a temporary period to
her sufferings, by giving the long-looked-for
nod, and they depart. She is standing alone
by an open window, leaning her fagged head
against the folded shutter, and trying to get
the sound of Bell's loud and amorous plea-
santries out of her ears, when she is aware
that Diana has stolen shyly up to her.

"Are you coming home to-morrow?" she
asks, looking diffidently round as if aware
that the magnificence of Joan's present surroundings has set a gulf between her and
her cousin. "I would not, if I were you;
I would stay as long as they asked me; it is
worse than ever at home. I think we quarrel
more and Sarah sweeps less. I wonder how
you will ever bear the change!"

Joan's leaden heart echoes the question.

"How, indeed?"

"You did not know that we were coming

to-night!" pursues Diana, with reddened cheeks and mortified eyes. "I saw it in your face the moment we came in; you looked so—so—surprised!"

"Did I?" cries Joan, remorsefully; aware that it is only regard for her feelings which has kept Diana from employing a stronger word.

"A man on horseback—a groom came soon after breakfast this morning," pursues Diana, putting up her hand to her head to feel whether Micky's banner still waves securely from her skull; "he brought a note from Mrs. Wolferstan; she said she hoped we would excuse the short notice and come to dinner to-night; of course" (in an ashamed tone), "I know that they did not want us *really*—of course we were only stop-gaps—some one else had failed them!"

Joan shakes her head dispiritedly.

"I do not know—I have not an idea!"

"How big our heads are!" says the other presently, in a discontented tone; "they are far the biggest in the room! Bell would have it that it was the fashion to put all sorts of things on one's head at once; she said that of course the fashion plate knew better than you! however" (with a sigh), "I daresay it does not matter! — I daresay no one notices!"

Miss Dering wishes from the bottom of her heart that she could echo this hope.

"I wish that Bell would not talk so loud, do not you?" goes on the girl in a lowered tone; "I heard her voice far above every one else's at dinner; some one told me that the young gentleman who took her in was a *lord!* was he really? I am sure that she thinks she has made quite a conquest; but I could see that he was only making fun of her!" a moment later in a tone of indignant apprehension, "mother has gone to sleep, do you see? her cap is all askew; I am so afraid that it may fall off altogether; do you think I might wake her without any one noticing?"

She steps softly away on this delicate

errand, and having succeeded in recalling her parent from the land of dreams, remains beside her to hinder her from returning thither.

On every previous evening of her visit, Wolferstan has, immediately on entering the room, made for Miss Dering as straight and as quickly as if he had been shot out of a cross-bow at her. He comes towards her to-night also ; but it seems to her sad fancy as if there were less alacrity in his step—in his eye a divided allegiance. He certainly glances once or twice towards the spot where Lalage, in Mrs. Wolferstan's arm-chair, of which she has nightly taken smiling but resolute pos-session, rests her lazy length, and displays

> "——the breast's superb abundance
> Where a man might base his head !"

" How pale you look !" he cries, discontentedly, coming up to Joan ; "are you fagged ?—overtired ? you must be to look so ! I never saw you so white !"

It is far from his intention to do so, but

there is something in his tone that conveys the impression that her pallor is not a becoming one.

"Am I pale?" she says, putting up her fingers to her cheeks, as if touch could tell her their tint; "I mostly am now!—I had a good colour once, had not I?—a milkmaid's cheeks; but" (sighing a little) "when everything else I had went, that went too! do not you think it was wise?"

"After all you are quite red enough!" he says, his eyes straying vexedly away to her three relations, and resting on Bell, who is languishing on an ottoman; two large and well-benzined shoes protruded before her, while the artillery of her eyes plays with incessant but unavailing fury on the distant and unheeding diplomat. "Did you know" (lowering his voice) "that they were to be here to-night?"

"I had not an idea, believe me!" she answers, hanging her head in utter downcastness.

"It is another of my mother's *surprises*," he says, with a short dry laugh.

Joan lifts her drooped head.

"Why did she ask them?" she says, in a low eager voice; "I have been puzzling my brain to find a reason; I am quite at a loss!"

"Are you?" he says, shortly and bitterly; "I am not!" then, a moment later, in a lighter tone, as if making an effort to get the better of his ill-humour; "have you discovered that I am extremely cross to-night?"

She smiles a little.

"I think I have, but do not be cross to-night; it is the last evening!—be cross to-morrow instead!"

He laughs more naturally.

"I have every intention of being cross to-morrow too!"

"Do, by all means!" she answers gravely; "that will not affect me."

He knits his forehead and looks puzzled.

"Not affect you! why not?"

" I have not the gift of second sight," she replies quietly, " I cannot—being in Black-shire — observe what your humours are in Scotland !"

His brow grows straight again.

" Oh, I see," he says, in a relieved voice. " To be sure, we are all going to Scotland to-morrow—all of us ; of course, of course. Do not you envy us ?"

In his eyes, so sombre and thwarted a moment ago, there is a gleam of pleasure and mischief.

" That I do," she answers wistfully ; " it is the first year since I can remember that I have ever missed going. Shall I ever see the moors—the amethyst-coloured evening heather again, I wonder ?" There is almost a sob in her voice as she speaks ; then, as if anxious to disguise and slur over her emotion, she adds quickly : " Miss Beauchamp is going to Scotland too, is not she ?"

" Miss Beauchamp too ; do you think we would leave her behind ?"

There is the same mirth in voice and eye which had before struck her with surprise.

"You will set off quite early, I suppose?" she says, trying by a cool and level tone to conceal the hurt that his light indifference does her. "At cock crow? before I am up? When I come down I shall find an empty house?"

"An empty house!" he repeats, but he speaks in such a stupid, absent, parrot-like tone that she sees he has not the faintest idea of what he is saying. Her glance following his, finds the explanation. It has returned to Lalage, who, looking at him with a laughing audacity over the top of her spread fan, is sending him unmistakable greetings and invitations with her saucy eyes. "Why is she beckoning to me?" he says fretfully; "she has been making signs to me for the last five minutes. What does she want? I shall pay no attention; there is no reason why I should, is there?"

"That is for you to decide," answers Joan,

a little coldly, while her heart, which, through the evening, has been steadily running down like an unwound clock, falls an inch or two lower still.

"I suppose I must too," he adds a moment later, rising from his seat; "perhaps she may really have something to say to me. I shall be back in a moment. Mind that you do not let any one take my place. There," playfully lifting a bit of her lowest flounce, and spreading it over the chair he has left. "There, if any one offers to usurp it, say that it is engaged." Smiling, he goes and walks quick and straight and comely across the room.

Joan's eyes and heart see him (though her ears cannot hear) asking for what he is wanted. The answer is apparently satisfactory, for he sits down. Is it worth while sitting down for one minute? The minute passes: lengthens itself to five—to ten. At the end of that time he rises. Is he coming back? The night is yet young; there may yet be a good farewell talk before them—a talk for her to live upon by-and-by. But no, Joan! not so; the evening is to be consistently painful to the end. He rises, indeed, but so does Lalage; and still talking, they saunter away into the conservatory, and are lost among the darkly shining orange-trees.

*   *   *   *   *

"Had not we better ring for our fly?" says Diana's anxious voice presently, breaking the silence of Joan's now desolate retreat; "our driver is the one that always gets drunk! But Bell will not hear of it;—she says that if we go so early they will think that we do not know what is what; but, I caught Mrs. Wolferstan giving *such* a yawn just now. I am sure that they are longing to be rid of us."

Joan shrugs her shoulders a little.

"Let them long!" she says dismally.

Something in her tone strikes Diana.

"Are you coming home to-morrow?" she asks, looking at her narrowly with kind and inquisitive eyes. " I would not, if I were you ; and have you enjoyed yourself really—— *really ?*"

" Yes, I have enjoyed myself," answers Joan slowly, while her eyes—a little misty— look dreamily away over Diana's head ; " certainly I have enjoyed myself," with emphasis, as if asseverating what another contradicted ; " and—yes, I shall come home to-morrow."

A few minutes later the drawing-room door-lock clicks gently, and a black figure flits along the lighted passages, and up the carven stairs Joan has stolen away to bed, but it is one o'clock in the morning before the Moberleys make their bows.

CHAPTER XXIV.

HE emptiness of a small house is nothing. Portland Villa empty, is, indeed, far to be preferred to Portland Villa full; but in the wide cold voidness of a large house there is something that weights the heart and pulls down the spirits.

So Joan feels when she comes downstairs next morning. She had fed, perhaps, a faint hope that some change of plan, some late-sleeping drowsiness, some mis-reading of Bradshaw's dark page may have detained at least one of the travellers. But no! In all

the broad and silent rooms, along all the
lengthy passages there is no voice nor any
step save those of the quiet-footed servants.
She breakfasts in absolute loneliness — worse
than loneliness, indeed—for being entirely
without appetite she is continually plied
by the butler with hot meats against which
her soul revolts, and crumpets which would
choke her.

It is, perhaps, unthrifty of her to neglect
the last chance of appetising food which,
humanly speaking, she is likely to have for
months, or perhaps years. It is certainly
unwise to run the risk of arriving hungry at
Portland Villa ; but the lovesick soul loathes
the honeycomb even more than the full one
does. By-and-by she goes heavily through
the walks, where hitherto she has never gone
alone. She says a separate good-bye to each
special resort—to the wood, to the trellised
rose walks, to the garden god. But she is
half sorry afterwards that she has done so,
for they none of them look the same.

There has been a heavy rain; the narrow wood-paths are drowned, and the strong brambles lay hold on her with rude wet hands—there is now no one to free her from them—the trellised roses are sodden, limp, and over-blown; sloppy tears are racing down the god's limbs and running down his nose. Then she packs up her clothes; packing a sigh between each gown; then at length Mrs. Wolferstan makes her tardy appearance.

"They were as nearly as possible late, I hear," she says, referring to her departed guests. "Anthony will always persist in allowing such a narrow margin, and Lalage is an inveterate dawdle! I cannot understand that; can you? I always say," (with her little January laugh), "I have only one virtue, but at least I have that in perfection. I am punctual; never to my knowledge did I keep anyone waiting in my life!"

And now Miss Dering is on her homeward road. The fourteen days are over—behind her instead of before. The carriage horses are drawing her back as cheerfully as they brought her. In her ears still ring her hostess's chill-toned farewell words:

"So glad to have made your acquaintance. I hope we shall have the pleasure of seeing you here again some day."

Some day! That is substantial food for a hungry heart, is not it? Before her mind's eye she still sees the tepid civility of Mrs. Wolferstan's good-bye smile. She has reached the gate of Portland Villa. The ragged string which ties gate and gatepost together, to the confusion of the Sardanapalus pigs, has twisted itself into a knot. The footman fumbles with it for ten minutes before he conquers it. But at last the carriage rolls in, rolls up to the door, and the footman boldly pulls the bell. Let him pull. Is it not broken?

On the seldom scoured doorstep the dogs' muddy paws have wrought many ingenious patterns—only to be erased, probably, by the action of time—and, also, on the doorstep crowd all the dogs themselves. Carriage company is not common at Portland Villa, and always wildly excites them. They will hardly let her get out, and when at last she has succeeded in descending amongst them, each greets her in his own fashion. Regy— a kind and conscientious dog, but not gifted with much insight into character—evidently mistakes her for his enemy the butcher's boy, who also arrives in a carriage, or at least a species of one. This is clear by the tone of his bark and the bristled roughness of his hostile back. Algy having smelt her carefully all over, so as to ensure not being led away by a superficial resemblance, gives her a temperate welcome, but Mr. Brown knows her in a minute. He trusts neither to his nose nor to his shortsighted eyes. His heart tells him that it is Joan. He is not quite so clean as could be wished, as he has clearly been indulging lately in the not uncommon luxury of a roll in the ashpit, but what his greeting wants in cleanliness it makes up in warmth. She stoops down and kisses him. He is certainly like Anthony's dog—a humble vulgarised likeness—but still like. Walking along beside her, almost entirely on his hind-legs, in a way which would make his fortune were he a professional dog, he escorts her into the drawing-room and introduces her to the family, for they are all three there; all with their backs turned to her and their noses flattened against the shut window, in eager and reverent survey of the departing Wolferstan equipage.

" If he has not left the gate untied !" cries Mrs. Moberley, in accents of high indignation ; " and now the pigs will be in before you can say ' Knife !' Just like a servant, anything to save themselves trouble !"

At the sound of Joan's step they all turn and greet her after their several manners, and so absorbing is the interest that her return occasions, that, though two minutes later the pigs, watching their opportunity, unlatch the gate and enter, numerous as talkative, they remain quite unnoticed and undisturbed.

" You were not asked to stay, I suppose ?" says Bell, with a laugh, as she stretches her copious form on the little couch, and prepares to take part, at luxurious ease, in high converse about the aristocracy.

Joan opens her blue eyes.

" *To stay!* how do you mean ? I stayed a fortnight."

" I meant for good, of course !" rejoins her cousin, still laughing, and with a playful emphasis on the two important words. " Anthony did not ask you to stay ?"

" Pooh ! pooh !" cries Mrs. Moberley chidingly ; " do not put notions into the girl's head ! it did not require spectacles to see which way the Colonel was looking ; I never made out her name, Joan ; that stout girl with a fresh colour—dear me ! she *was* stout ! she beat you, Bell !"

" She looked one of the Upper Ten all the

same !" replies Bell ; " after all you cannot
mistake them !"

" I cannot say that you look much the
better for your out !" says Mrs. Moberley,
re-seating upon her nose the spectacles which,
pushed up on her forehead, have been enjoying a season of rest and inaction ; and regarding her niece somewhat narrowly through
them. " I daresay all those kickshaws did
not agree with you ; after all there is nothing
like a plain roast joint with the gravy in it ;
all the doctors tell you so !"

" How low you must feel !" says Bell,.
pensively ; " I can sympathize with you ; I
feel as flat as flat myself this morning ! that
is the worst of that kind of society ; it spoils
you for all other !"

" Speak for yourself !" cries Diana, in her
high honest voice, while her healthy cheeks
take a deeper tinge than even youth, country
air, and a good digestion, have given them ;
" as for me, I never spent such a wretched
evening in my life ! I do not know which I

was most ashamed of—myself, or you, or mother!—what fishes out of water we looked! —now did not we, Joan?"

Miss Dering is delivered from the delicate dilemma in which this question places her, by Mrs. Moberley, who makes a peaceable diversion by saying :

"Talking of fishes, I do wish, Joan, that you could get us the recipe of that sauce they served with the mullet last night; I declare I see no reason why Jane should not try her hand at it; of course you know old Mrs. Wolferstan well enough by this time not to mind mentioning it to her; indeed, many people take it as a compliment to be asked for their recipes!"

Joan gives a sort of gasp. Perhaps it is the confined atmosphere of the room — the Moberleys are not fond of air, and the window is closed—which makes her do so. It is the last straw which breaks the camel's back, though under many of the previous ones it has been cracking; and (although in reading of it, the cause seems absurdly disproportioned to the effect) at the request for the fish sauce recipe, she feels as if she must begin sobbing —begin and never stop.

"I hope you will not take it unkind of us," pursues Mrs. Moberley presently, placidly flowing away from her subject and into a new one; "if we leave you all alone the first night of your coming home : but, to tell the truth, we have been engaged for a week past to go on a little jaunt to-night!—well, I suppose it is a dance really, though they do not call it so—a sort of little friendly frisk got up among the young people—no doubt" (with a jolly laugh) "we shall have plenty of fun and quizzing!"

"It is at a place five miles the other side of Helmsley!" explains Diana; and in her eyes also there is a flash of young joy and expectant mirth ; "everybody about here has joined to hire the big omnibus from the King's Head ; it is to come here first : then we go round the town collecting everybody, we end with the Barracks : six of them have promised to come ; do you think " (a little doubtfully) " that it *can* hold us all ?"

" The Simpsons have offered mother a seat in their fly!" cries Bell, in glorious antistrophe; " otherwise she would have been obliged to walk " (laughing) ; " we set our faces against having one chaperone with us—nothing but officers and young ladies ! I am sure I cannot think how we shall all fit in !"

Joan gives a great sigh of relief. The text-like proverb which nine out of every ten people imagine to inhabit the Bible, " God tempers the wind to the shorn lamb," recurs vividly to her mind. If in a whole long evening of solitude, common sense, reflection, and strict self-schooling, she cannot get the better of the past, and offer a brave front to the future, she must be a poor creature indeed.

*   *   *   *   *

They are gone now. Mrs. Moberley has joggled heavily away in the Simpsons' fly, and the girls have bumped and rattled smartly off, in the as yet empty omnibus. Joan has done her duty by them all to the last : she has fastened on Mrs. Moberley's cap so straight and firm that no ordinary slumber can unseat it; she has dressed Diana's crisp hair, and discouraged the re-appearance in it of the bird of paradise; she has wisely left Arabella wholly alone, and allowed her to effloresce, unremonstrated with, into copious blue beads, pink flowers, and red fruit. She has kissed them all—Diana twice —and hoped they would enjoy themselves, and sweetly thanked them for their kind wish that she were about to accompany them.

They are gone ; Mrs. Moberley's last indistinct mandate screamed out of the fly window dies, drowned among the rolling of the wheels and the barking of the dogs. All of it that survives to reach Joan's ears, is the word "pigs!"

CHAPTER XXV.

"Can he prize the tainted posies
  Which on every breast are worn,
That may pluck the virgin roses
  From their never touched thorne?
        I can goe rest
        On her sweet brest;
That is the pride of Cynthia's train.
        Then stay thy tongue,
        Thy mermaid song
Is all bestowed on me in vain."

JOAN is left alone with her trouble —a trouble that, by its nature, rebuts sympathy; and which would be centupled were anyone—even the dogs—to conjecture its existence. After all it is not always our legitimate sorrows—the sorrows for which our friends condole with us on black-edged paper, and, to assuage which, they ply us with salvolatile and texts—that sting us the most sharply. Joan takes her sorrow out of doors, and sits down with it on the base of the sundial. She sits down, nor is it by any means clear when she will be able to get up again; as three of the dogs, who prefer her soft gown to either the chill stone or the damp grass, and who know too well what good manners and sociability are to go back to the drawing-room without her, have pinned her to earth by disposing their warm plump bodies upon her. Her meditations are set to the music of their snores. The soft shod night comes stepping on with her soundless feet: the lush long grass, the weedy gravel path, the leggy scarlet geraniums, and lean slatternly rose-bushes, are growing indistinct.

The Campidoglio children are enjoying one farewell riot among their cabbages and clothes-lines before going to bed.

" Let me look it in the face!" she says,
half under her breath ; " I am crying for the
moon, and I am sickly and dolorous and
unstrung, because it does not fall into my
lap—because it prefers to go on shining up
above me,"—a moment later—"up above me!
no! the metaphor does not hold there; in
my feeling for him there is nothing of looking
up ; perhaps of us two, I am the more to be
looked up to ; though indeed in neither is
there much to reverence!" A longer pause.
The angry Campidoglio mother has swept
away her offspring; there is no sound but a
slight snore now and then from Mr. Brown,
as his nose lies comfortably in the palm of
Joan's hand. Even at Portland Villa there
is privacy and peace. Forgetting Mr. Brown,
she has now flung her arms round the sundial.
Her face is pressed close against the hard
cold stone. There is no one to hear the drip
of her hot tears.

" Oh my dear!" she says in a low and
sobbing whisper; " I do love you! it is no

use now to think whether it would have been better to leave it alone; it is too late! the thing is done; though I pray God to give me strength to hide it from you as long as I live. . . . I have loved you without your bidding me; it is not very wise of me, is it? but after all there is nothing to be so much ashamed of! my love will do you no harm if it is good of its kind; I think it is good! —I think it is good!—it may even profit you a little! in all this world, hearty, wholesome, clean love never did anything but good either to the giver or the taker; after all it is but a poor huckstering kind of love that insists on getting as much as it gives; it is not love, if it stickles for an equivalent, it is barter!"

After a pause, her head still leant against the stone; her arms still embracing the cold pillar: "I will go on loving you, dear—*will!*"

-(with a sad low laugh)—"as if there were any choice in the matter—as if I could help it—but I will not let you spoil my life: you shall not make a peevish sluggard of me: I will sleep, I will eat, I will laugh, I will help other people. I will be the better, not the worse, for having loved you!"

She lifts her wet eyes to the sky—(at any high or worthy thought one naturally looks upwards, even if it be only to a white-washed ceiling)—to the sky, where now all the silver squadrons of the old old stars are drawn up in their nightly array; but alas! between her and their heavenly mild shining, thrusts itself the eager human beauty of her love's face; in her ears she still hears his voice, naming to her, as it did two nights ago, one after one, the Constellations' lovely names. She looks quickly down again, and her gaze, moistened and moved, falls on the dusk forms of the Sardanapalus pigs moving dimly about in the adjoining field, and occasionally grunting shortly and comfortably to each other, as they snout and rout to and fro, hither and thither. She may look at the pigs as long as she pleases. There is no link that binds them and Wolferstan together in her mind.

The heavy dews of late summer fall round her; they moisten the soft silk of her hair, and the fabric of her gown; Mr. Brown is shivering in his sleep. A bat—voiceless elfin creature—circles fearlessly round her, crediting her with no more life than the stone against which she leans, when suddenly, in a moment, he is disabused, for she has sprung to her feet, scattering like dead leaves the three solid dogs who had been making a mattress of her. After all, her ears are sharper than theirs.

It is not yet ten o'clock, so the dawn cannot yet be coming, nor have the stars multiplied their shafts of light, and yet—to Joan's eyes—how light it has suddenly grown! For has not her sun risen?

Wolferstan is beside her: Wolferstan—the departed—the meekly forsworn—the prayed against. Even in this dark place she can see the happy flashing of his young and passionate eyes.

"You are not gone to Scotland?" she cries

all in a minute; and out of her hurrying words and shaken tones she has much ado to keep the sudden joy that is sweeping in high tide over her so lately stranded heart.

"How do you know that?" he asks with a low laugh of young content; "how do you know that I am not an optical delusion? It is almost too dark to see you; but I hear that you are breathing quickly! Are you frightened? Will you make sure that I am real?"

As he speaks, he stretches out his right hand to her, but she does not take it.

"Why have you come back?" she asks in the same sudden voice, and with the same short quick breath.

"I have not come back!" he answers laughing, "because I never went; I never meant to go; you told me that I was going, and I was too polite to contradict you; I have been in London all day—I could not get away before. No, I have not gone to Scotland—why should I?"

She laughs nervously, and her eyes avoid meeting the dusk fond shining of his.

"Why do people go to Scotland ?—to shoot grouse, to catch salmon, to stalk deer !"

He shrugs his broad shoulders, and stretches out his hands with a gesture of abnegation.

"I renounce them all !"

"And Miss Beauchamp ?" says Joan, her eyes still bent on the dim shapes of the shivering discomfortable dogs, and the almost invisible grass, and speaking with pursed lips and a little stiff tone ; "has she not gone, either ?"

"Of course she has gone !" he cries, giving a petulant stamp ; "why will you persist in always bracketing us together ? I shall repent of having told you that episode of my infancy, if you will persist in so continually and basely throwing it in my teeth."

"Have you come to tell me the sequel of it ?" she asks in a voice which, though a little mollified, contains still a good deal of starch.

"Why do you ask these offensive ques-

tions !" he cries impatiently. " I wish I had
a box of cigar-lights that I might strike a
Vesuvian and see whether your face tallies
with your cold east-windy voice. It is evident that you are displeased with me—and
why ?—is it because of—last night ?—because
of—because of the—the—conservatory ?"

As he speaks, shying a little, perhaps, at
the last words, he takes her hand. He has
some little difficulty in finding it, as it is
hanging down by her side, and there is small
light to help him ; but perhaps she covertly
aids him, for before long it is lying small,
cool, and entirely passive in his.

" Let us hear the worst !" he says, half
laughing, yet earnestly. " No—I will not
let it go"—(as she makes a puny effort to
withdraw her fingers)—" I have done nothing
to deserve having it taken away from me ; if
I had I would give it back to you in a moment !—but come, let us hear—what do you
suppose happened ?—what do you think we
said or did—when we got there ?"

"I have never hazarded a conjecture!" she answers, lifting her small white chin into the air, and speaking in a tone of equal frostiness and falsity.

"Do you think—do you think," he says stammering, and, dark as it is, she knows that he is reddening; "do you think" (in a sneaky and uncertain voice), "that I *kissed* her?"

"I think it is extremely probable!" (in a tone, that, but for the tremble in it, would be the *ne plus ultra* of virginal dignity and ice). She fears that her fingers are trembling too, and that he can feel them.

"How about the charity that thinketh no evil?" cries the young man joyously. "Well then!—you are wrong!—I did nothing of the kind!"

"You did not?" (the frost disappearing in an instantaneous thaw, melted by the sunshine of an ungoverned relief and joy).

"I did not!—to you" (in a slower and less triumphant key), "to you, who are my conscience, to whom I have always persistently turned my worst side outwards—I will not deny—if it were not dark I do not think that I should be brave enough to confess this—that it *was* a temptation ; I suppose there never yet was a storm that did not leave some sort of a swell behind it, however entirely the storm itself may be past—well " (speaking quicker and more easily), " I am afraid that I can count on my fingers the temptations that I have resisted in the course of my life ; but I did resist this one !—as I live I did !"

She has snatched away her hand from him, successfully this time, and still standing, throws her arms round her old friend the dial. Perhaps she is thankful for its cold support.

" Even if I had," continues the young fellow eagerly, in some repentance for, and some fear at the results of his own candour ; " even if I had it would not have hurt—it would not have touched my utter loyalty to you !—you do not comprehend ? ah ! we are made of a coarser

pâte than you ! the sort of feeling that I have
for her, you would not take at a gift—you
would toss it away disdainfully were I to offer
it to you ! There is no doubt" (in a tone of
irritated reflection), " that some women have
the happy knack of stirring up and bringing
to the surface the dregs of one's being ; now,
with you, I forget that I have any dregs !"

No answer. Regy and Algy have seated
themselves very close together on the foot of
the sundial, propped against each other in
dismal community of endurance and looking
ostentatiously miserable.

" When I came back," continues Wolferstan, repenting still more heartily of his
honesty ; " it was in ten minutes — believe
me it was in ten minutes—you were gone !
I went out on the terrace, I ran to all our
resorts—to our trellised rose-walk—to our
beech-tree seat—to our yew hedge—you were
nowhere ; I called you softly by your dear
little quaint name—did you ever hear of such
impertinence ?—but there came no answer ;

and at last, some one told me that you had gone to bed ! why did you go to bed ? what business had you to go ? who gave you leave ?"

Still she is silent. The small night wind blows her heavy gown softly against him, but carries no message to him from her dumb mouth.

" Are you still out of humour with me ?" he asks, rather crest-fallen; then, after a moment, in a tone of doubtful exultation, " Is it possible, Joan—is it possible that you are—jealous of me ? It seems too good news to be true; but, indeed—indeed it looks like it. As for me, do you know that I am jealous of the very dews that have leave to drench your gown ? of the very dial round which your arms are thrown ; why are they— why are they not round me instead ? at least, I should not be so cold and unresponsive." He steps nearer to her, with his arms passionately outstretched, but she slips from him as if she were a mist-maiden, made out of moonbeams and evening vapour. "Are you angry?" he cries vehemently; "indeed you have no need to be! I ask you to put your dear arms round me for always—for all my life, be it short or long! Oh, more than ever now I hope it may be long!"

She does not answer, but it is not wrath that keeps her dumb, nor does he any longer think so, for through the gloom her fair wet eyes have met the dark fond burning of his.

"I had to come to-night," he says in an eager half-whisper; "I could not put it off till to-morrow. I thought, 'I may die in the night.' Even if they had all been here—they are all out, are not they, God bless them!—but even if they had all been sitting round I think I should have had to have asked you all the same."

She laughs a little—a laugh that is half a sob.

"I meant to have asked you last night, only you went to bed," indignantly. "The more I reflect upon it the more unjustifiable I think it

of you. By going to bed you robbed us of a
whole long day—a whole twenty-four hours!
How *dared* you?"

He has taken her two arms and laced them
about his neck; with his own he is straitly
prisoning her supple sweet body. She is not
struggling at all; why should one struggle to
escape from absolute well-being? After a
moment:

" Have you reflected," she says sobbingly,
" that you will have to sit opposite to me at
breakfast for perhaps fifty years?"

" I will do nothing of the kind," he answers
stoutly; " opposite to you with a long table,
an urn, and half a dozen other impediments
between us! No, no, I have had enough of
sitting opposite to you! I will never sit
opposite to you again. Oh, my one love!
my sweetheart, my tall white lily-bud, how
soon are you going to give me a kiss?"

At his speech she slowly raises her silk
head, which has been drooping lily-wise on
his breast, and lifting her passionate pure

mouth to his, their lips make sweet acquaintance in an interminable first kiss. Does any
after kiss, I wonder, ever equal, in point of
mere duration, the enormous longevity of a
first one? Only the stars and the dogs see it.
The stars, both the great and the small ones;
both those that shine in luminous solitude, and
those that are gathered in lustrous families.
As for the dogs, they look away yawning and
humping up their chilly backs. To Joan it is
an absolutely new sensation; to Wolferstan—
well—not wholly novel. But this goes without saying; a man brings his scanty dregs,
and a woman her ripe first-fruits, and all the
world (the woman herself included) look upon
it as a fair and equitable exchange. In an
innocent tumult of great and astonished bliss,
Joan gives herself to her love's new caresses.
He is the first to break the lovely silence.

"What is it that gives this sharpest edge
of keen pain-pleasure?" he cries, looking passionately up at the impassioned sky. "Oh,
love! do you know that I can fancy no

ecstasy in the conventional idea of heaven?
the dead-sweet certainty of everlasting fruition
would nauseate my palate; it is the uncertainty—the thought that you may die—that
I may die—that to-morrow—to-morrow it
may be ended and gone, that makes this
agony of rapture."

As he speaks he gathers yet more strain-
ingly and closely her trembling body to his
young and leaping heart, but at his words she
shudders, and draws herself away.

"You are wrong! you are wrong!" she
cries vehemently; "in love there is no uncertainty. All those who have ever really
loved, whether they died to-day or three
thousand years ago, love still. Oh, my dear!
what good or pleasure could there be in it if
we believed that it could pass? In this weak
and shifting world it is the one all-sure, all-
strong, all-lovely thing! Kill me, sooner
than convince me of its mortality!"

As she so brokenly speaks, she lifts her
streaming eyes to the stars that are not

clearer or more holy than they. And those words and that look her lover carries away with him in his heart, when, five minutes later, she sweetly but resolutely sends him away. I think that they will be buried with him when he dies.

CHAPTER XXVI.

HE French call a wakeful night a "*nuit blanche.*" Surely this is a misnomer. To most people, a night on which they do not sleep is a black, not a white one. But for once, in Joan's case, the epithet is meet and fitting. The night that follows her troth-plight is one of the whitest of her life. And yet she sleeps not at all. Why should she? Sleep is a good and goodly thing, better than any jog-trot happiness, or usual every day content, but it is not better than a great keen and poignant felicity. Why should she then exchange the better for the worse? Broad awake she lies; not tossing about, not feverish or troubled; quite still and restful, with her two white hands clasped beneath her head, and her wide blue eyes looking her new treasure full and steadily in the face. She is unconscious even of the flinty pillow and the potato-stuffed mattress. She hears every one of the slowly told hours as they are spoken out to the night by the hospital clock. She hears her aunt and cousins return; hears them trail wearily upstairs; hears Bell say something loud about "Jackson;" and Diana, mindful of her supposed slumbers, cry "Hush!" Mrs. Moberley, indeed, goes so far as creakily to open her (Joan's) bedroom-door, and look in, shading the candle-flame with four fat fingers; but in a moment, Joan has shut her eyes, and feigned the sleep that is so far from her brain.

"Fast as a church! sound as a top!" says her aunt in a large whisper; and so closes the noisy door again, and retires.

By and by, the morning draws on. She is
in no hurry for it. She is content to lie and
watch it slowly supplanting its ebon-haired
sister; to see the dawn-wind sucking in, and
then blowing outwards again the scant curtain
at the open window; to see the eastern gates
painting themselves with pearl against the
coming of the great flame horses that will

"Shake the darkness from their loosened manes,
And beat the twilight into flakes of fire."

They have come now: they are stretching
in mighty gallop through the sky: the sun
has risen, and Joan must rise too; for have
not she and her love given each other early
tryst by the washing of the morning waves.
She dresses and warily goes down the dark
stairs; warily, for, in all human probability,
a coal box or pail of water at the stair foot
awaits all those whose steps are not guided
by a crafty and distrustful caution. The
house is dark and shut up and close. She
gropes her way to the dining-room shutters

and opens them.   After all it would have
been kinder perhaps to have left them shut.
An overset chair, empty soda-water bottles,
crumbs, sandwich-wrecks, mark where the
family have sparsely revelled over-night.   It
is the same scene of squalor, as that to which
she had descended on the first morning of
her arrival; but with how different an eye
does she now regard it!   In her glance there
is no heart sickness, no inward shrinking from
the prospect of a limitless future of dirt.
From all these evils she is about to be
delivered; and this deliverance—great and
joy-bringing as it would be were it taken
singly, is only one small incident in her large
felicity.

Through the reaped harvest-fields her swift
feet carry her, hardly feeling the weight of
her light body; the fields where now, of all
the sappy green blades that greeted her eyes
on that first April morning of her coming,
nothing now remains but pale harsh stubble.
The dogs pursue each other in foolish

scampering circles over the plain where, so
lately, the crowded ears waved and rustled
as high as a man's head. As she nears the
sea, she quickens her pace ; for—early as she
is, and no mock modesty, or thought of
enhancing her own value by delay has made
her late—yet he is before her. There he
stands among the sandy dunes, looking
towards the east and her. As she comes
stepping towards him, over the faint sea
hollies, and the bitter wan sea grass, she
seems to him a transfigured Joan. Surely
her cheeks have borrowed some of the fine
dawn red that lined the sun's cradle ; surely
her eyes have stolen some of the heavenly
shining. So, in the eye of the morning they
meet, and give each other a sweet good-
morrow.

"Are you sure," says Joan by and by,
gently yet deftly eluding her lover's blandish-
ments, and soberly taking his hand instead ;
"are you sure that you are in the same mind
still ? are you sure that it was not—was not

—accidental last night? that there is no—no
—mistake?"

He laughs—a low laugh, less of mirth than
of utter heart content. "There is a mistake!"
he says cheerfully, " or at least there was one
—I have been repenting of it ever since last
night. Do you know what it is?—That I
did not ask you to marry me the first time,
—the first moment—I ever saw you. What
a great deal of time we have wasted in pre-
liminaries!" (regretfully); " but," (in a lighter
tone), "never mind, there is plenty still
before us; in all human likelihood there are
yet many good years ahead of us. More, far
more, than we have yet passed."

She shakes her head a little sadly. " In
life and in death there is no likely or unlikely :
the likely go ; the unlikely stay."

They have sat down on almost the same
spot, where, five months or more ago, he had
found her sitting alone, with clasped knees
and far travelling eyes. Over the sea there is
spread a wide and luminous mist—gold-shot,

like a king's vesture ; and above it, trampling
it with his fire-feet, chariots the great sun,
making all earth and heaven one laugh.

" But seriously," says Joan, putting her
arms round Mr. Brown, and arranging him
quietly between herself and her lover, as a
slight barrier against the latter's insatiate en-
dearments, " but seriously, *indeed* I am not
asking for the sake of being contradicted. I
never was more deeply in earnest in my life.
Have you well and ripely considered the
many and great drawbacks that there un-
doubtedly are to me ?"

" What drawbacks ?" he says abruptly,
colouring and throwing out at her a side-
glance of embarrassment and fear.

She laughs softly. " You need not look
so tragic ; I know of no new ones, only the
old ones—with which you are quite as well
acquainted as I am !"

" Is that all ?" he says, while his chest rises
and then sinks again, in a great sigh of relief.
" Well, let us hear them ! Which be they ?"

"Have you reflected," says Joan slowly, and flushing a little, while with her bare palm she scoops up a few grains of loose sea sand, "that you will be Mrs. Moberley's nephew?"

He nods. "Yes—Mrs. Moberley's nephew. Has she any more? or am I the only one?"

"That you will be Bell's first cousin?" still more slowly and, bending face and eyes as if to count the sand-grains in her hand. "Not *second*, mind—one may slur over second cousins—but *first*?"

Again he nods. "Yes—Bell's first cousin —go on!"

"That they will call you Anthony? At least I do not know about Diana, but I think that my aunt, and I am sure that Bell will."

If, at this suggestion, Wolferstan's spirit undergoes any inward convulsion is known only to himself and his conscience. Narrowly as Joan is now watching him, she can detect no sign of wincing. "I shall be hurt if they do not!" he answers doughtily. "If it would give them any satisfaction to abbreviate me to 'Tony,' I am sure that they are more than welcome."

"That you will have to be 'hail fellow well met' with Micky — why do I call him Micky?" (impatiently correcting herself); "it is a bad habit I have fallen into—with Mr. Brand and Mr. Jackson—"

"And Mr. Brown!" interrupts Wolferstan joyously, pulling that gentleman's left ear. "Do you hear, Mr. Brown? you and I are to be 'hail fellow well met'—so give us a paw."

Mr. Brown complies, and not being a dog to do things by halves, he rapidly gives first one paw then the other, and finally jumps wholly up on Wolferstan's knee, where he sits with difficulty poising himself, but trying to look comfortable and smirking on that uneasy eminence.

She shakes her head with a little hopeless gesture.

"I see that you will not be grave!"

"Why should I be?" cries Wolferstan,

bubbling over again with unavoidable young
laughter. "No one could make so bad a
joke to-day, that I should not laugh at it, but
indeed I am grave sometimes. Last night—
by-the-by, did you sleep last night? I think
I shall be rather hurt if you tell me that you
did—I did not close my eyes. I heard all
the clocks—I really believe we have twenty
that strike, besides several loud tickers that
do not strike—well, I heard them beat out
every quarter of an hour of the tardy night.
I could not sleep for plans that jostled each
other in my head—ten lives will not be long
enough for all the work that I mean to crowd
into mine—into *ours* I mean!" with a happy
quick changing of the lonely for the com-
panionable pronoun.

She does not interrupt or answer him with
words, but the eager shining of her eyes tells
with how keen a sympathy she follows him.

"Do you know," he says, quite gravely
now, though to-day his gravity is almost as
joyous as his laughter; "do you know that

I have slouched and dawdled through twenty-seven years of my life?—is not that enough in all conscience?—for myself I have never had any ambition: always I have needed some one either to goad or to coax me into real work; hitherto there has been no one—no one to do either!—they say now-a-days, that there is no such person as the devil, do not they?—well, all I know is, that I have a special own devil of sloth and sluggardliness! —beloved, you will help me to fight him, will not you?"

"That I will, God willing!" she says, low but steadfastly, while her fingers straitly yet modestly press the nervous hand that, clasping hers, rests on Mr. Brown's warm back; he having jumped down from Wolferstan's knee, and resumed his position between the lovers as soon as he thought he could do so without hurting the young man's feelings.

"Among all the women I have ever loved," says Wolferstan, lifting his confident bold eyes to the kind suave sky above him; "and"

(laughing), " indeed their name is Legion—
there has never been one that inspired me
with a wish to *rise !*—always I have felt quite
comfortable and high enough, while you,
beloved — already — already you begin to
beckon me up to your own level !"

" To my own level ?" she cries, in eager
quick disclaimer, while her eyes go to meet
his through a lovely mist ; " nay, love, higher
—higher !"

For a few moments both are silent. The
tide is ebbing fast. The wave that frothed
at their feet ten minutes ago, now sucks the
glorious wet sand a hundred yards off, and
lends ever new lengths of shining sea ribbon
to the beach, to be fetched back again when
the next tide flows. Up and down, up and
down on the small bright billows, the fearless
sea mews ride.

" We will live to a great age !" says Wolferstan presently, quite seriously ; " I believe
that nine out of every ten people die because
they have not a resolute enough grip upon

life—because they are not determined to live !
—there is no reason, is there, why, this day
fifty years, we should not again be sitting here
still hand in hand—still looking out young-
hearted on the everlasting laughter of the
morning sea ?"

*   *   *   *   *

Early as it is when they met, it is nearly
one o'clock before they part; before, with a
hundred leave-takings, and as many moans,
Wolferstan grudgingly lets go, for half a dozen
hours, the woman whom he has done without
for seven and twenty contented years. On
very slight encouragement he would come to
luncheon ; but he does not receive that slight
encouragement. On the contrary, he is
strongly discouraged when he not obscurely
hints his willingness to share the Moberley
fare. Perhaps what gives firmness and con-
stancy to Joan's denial is the fact that she is
aware of what the luncheon is to consist; viz,
of a resurrection pie, in which all the atrocities

of the past week hold dreadful rendezvous in one abominable pasty.

On entering the drawing-room she finds the Moberley triad all gathered in the window; all standing, and all with heads close together bent over some object of interest held in the hands of one of them. At her entry they all turn with exclamations of relief and pleasure towards her.

"What a provoking girl you are!" cries Bell, sharply; "you always manage to be out of the way when anything interesting happens! here is another note come for you from the Abbey!—what can it mean?— surely" (in accents of almost indignation), "they cannot be wanting you back there already!—it cannot be another invitation!"

"An invitation! tut!" cries Mrs. Moberley; "more likely it is to tell her that she has left a pocket-handkerchief or a pair of stockings behind her!—girls are always so heedless about their linen!"

"That groom will know his way here

soon!" says Bell, with a proud smile; "the traffic between the two houses is certainly becoming brisk!"

During the foregoing observations Joan has torn open the well-fingered and stretched envelope presented to her, and hastily mastered its contents.

"It is not an invitation!" she says, answering the six intent eyes that are focussing her; and, if they had leisure to notice her complexion they might mark how utterly that small piece of note paper has abolished from her cheeks the dainty red that love, sea-air, and exercise, had printed there; "on the contrary, it is to say that Mrs. Wolferstan is coming here to-day, she will be here about three!"

"Mrs. Wolferstan?"

"Coming here?"

"To-day?" cry the three voices, in each of which awe, astonishment, and rapture, are mixed in differing proportions.

In Mrs. Moberley's the awe predominates;

in Diana's the astonishment; in Arabella's the rapture.

"Who was right now?" she cries triumphantly; "did not I tell you that we had made a favourable impression the other night, though you would have it that they were laughing at us — I always knew that it was only the ice that wanted breaking; who knows most of the world now, pray?"

"What a pity that the bell is broke!" says Mrs. Moberley, with meditative regret; "however, Sarah must be on the look out, and run before he has time to ring."

"I wish that she had chosen any other day to have a face ache!" says Diana, fretfully; "she looks so dreadful with her head tied up!"

"I am afraid," says Joan slowly, looking deprecatingly from one to the other of her three auditors; "that this is not exactly an ordinary visit; very likely—no doubt indeed she will call upon you some other day—by and by; but I think—I am afraid—that to-day she wishes to see me in private on some—some matter of business!"

"Do you mean," cries Bell loudly (anger deepening still more the already deep tone of her face), "that she expects us to turn out of our own drawing-room for *her*?—if she had wished to have any private conversation with you, why could not she send for you up to the Abbey? and, after all, what *can* she have to say to you that she does not wish your own *nearest relations* to hear?"

"I am sure that I do not want to hear her secrets!" says Mrs. Moberley placidly, though with a slight accent of disappointment; "I always hate mysteries!—from a girl I always was a terrible blab; I never could keep anything to myself; now, your poor aunt—*your* poor mother I mean, Joan, was quite different —she was as close as the grave; I defy anybody to get anything out of *her* that she did not want them to know!"

Ten minutes later, Joan, escaped from her family's conjectures and lamentations, is sitting in her own little bare room. On her knee is outspread her future mother-in-law's missive, which, for the tenth time, she is re-reading; although at the first she had mastered not only the gist, but every little word of it. And, indeed, there is not much to master.

"DEAR MISS DERING,

"If I hear nothing to the contrary I shall be with you this afternoon at three o'clock, as I wish to speak to you on a subject of the most vital importance.

"Yours truly,

"SOPHIA WOLFERSTAN."

What that subject of most vital importance is, Joan has no difficulty in conjecturing. And since, in less than two hours, a battle is to be fought, she is already arming herself with spear, shield, and buckler, for it. In order to harden herself against, and take the sting out of the many depreciating remarks that she is aware will, during the next three hours, be addressed to her; she is saying them all over, in order, to herself.

"I am poor!" she says, her eyes pensively fixed on the bald old drugget, whose original tints conjecture alone can now restore; "very poor!—I have no money—at least, I have a thousand pounds, which, in their eyes, is the same as having none; I have extremely undesirable connections — relations rather : I have sunk to a grade of society far below their or my own natural level. To all these accusations I must say unfeignedly 'Amen!'"

She sighs heavily, and her eyes raise themselves from the drugget to the washhand-stand, and fasten upon the mutilated ewer, which is now, so to speak, reduced to being only a torso; its handle having lately gone to join his long-lost brother, the spout, on the ash-heap. She smiles sardonically. "Certainly it is a singular house in which to come to look for a wife!" By and by, in self defence, she begins diffidently to reckon up her counterbalancing advantages. "I am well-born and well-bred," she says, half aloud; "I have an old and stainless name—older, more stainless than their own: there are absolutely no dark stories about any of us; we have always held our heads up, and looked the world straight in the face: as for me, I thank God that there is no man on this earth that can say the least light word of me; I thank God too, that I am healthy and strong: I bring no taint of disease or shame into any family I enter!"

As she so speaks, her dejected head lifts itself, her bent figure grows straight; there comes a greater dignity and confidence into her whole bearing.

"Let her say her worst!" she says, with low energy; "she shall not part us two!"

Strong in this resolution, she goes down to

luncheon; and every mouthful of resurrection pie confirms her in the resolve not
lightly to forego a lover in whose power it
is to deliver her for ever from so noisome a
plat.

CHAPTER XXVII.

THE Hospital-clock has reached only the second stroke of three, when the Wolferstan carriage draws up at the door of Portland Villa. Such unexampled punctuality utterly routs and consternates this simple household. Sarah, who, to do her justice, had meant to lay aside her face-cloth, and appear in the modified dirt of her Sunday cap, has no leisure to put her good intentions into practice; nor is she indeed in time to hinder the footman from tugging several times with wasted vigour at the broken bell-pull.

There is a sound of scuffling and hustling, as the Moberley family transplants itself hastily and repiningly from the drawing-room to the dining-room. Only Joan is ready. She has dusted the ornaments—so called—and the paralytic chairs (but this indeed she does every day), and has set about what flowers she could find in the ragged garden, to do honour to Anthony's mother. But when all her ameliorations are completed the apartment still appears to her to exhibit the *ne plus ultra* of lacquered dirt and gilt squalor.

The last Moberly skirt is scarcely out of sight when Sarah announces in a garbled and malaprop manner, " Mrs. Wolferstan," and the next instant, Joan and her mother-in-law-to-be stand face to face.

" Punctual to the moment, you see !" says the latter, beginning to talk at once and quickly; " did not I tell you that punctuality was my one virtue ? Never in all my life have I missed an appointment, or been late for a train; it is well to have

even a small virtue in perfection; is not
it ?"

"Is it a small virtue?" says Joan politely.
Through the affected gaiety of her guest's
manner she detects with surprise the nervous-
ness of her voice, and of as much of her face
as the white gauze veil, tightly swathed across
it, leaves visible. ("She must be going to say
something extremely disagreeable," is the
girl's reflection; "it frightens even herself;
well, it cannot be worse than what I have already said to myself!") "I am so sorry that
there is no blind," she says civilly, glancing
towards the shadeless casement; "and I am
afraid that the curtains do not draw very well
either. If I had known that you were coming,
I would have tried to rig up something."

But Mrs. Wolferstan does not heed her
remark.

"It is always a mistake beating about the
bush, is not it?" she says, laughing nervously,
and blinking in the potent sunlight which is
rolling the afternoon might of his fire-streams

in upon the counterfeit gold of her hair, and
the real lace on her dress; "always better to
go to the point at once—straight to the point
—I always go straight to the point; do not
you?—and I have always credited you with
such sound sense—give me good serviceable
work-a-day sense, that is what I always say;
and while you were with us, you and I found
out so many points of sympathy and agreement, did not we? that I have no doubt—
none at all—that—that—when I explain myself, we shall be found to agree perfectly
here, too."

"Perhaps, when I know what it is that we
are to agree upon, I shall be better able to
judge," answers Joan, with a grave smile.

She has sat down on a chair near, but not
too near to her companion; for Mrs. Wolferstan is not fond of being closely looked into,
and it is always the truest kindness to her to
seat oneself at about a bowshot's distance
from her.

"No doubt it is only a piece of silly servants'-hall tittle-tattle," continues the other, her uneasiness plainly waxing as she nears the pith of her subject; "we all know how things grow in the carrying—the proverbial three crows—ha! ha!—but I said, I will go to the fountain-head—it is always safest to go to the fountain-head; do not you agree with me?"

"Perfectly."

"I am quite inclined to laugh at myself already!" (still with the same factitious falsetto mirth) "you will laugh at me too—I give you leave—we will have a good laugh together; but the truth is—I am always an advocate for truth—truth, truth, at any price, I always say; well, the truth is, I came to speak to you about—about—*Anthony!*"

"You are too late!" says Joan, rising and stretching out her hands before her, as one that warns off another, and speaking in a resolute clear voice: "you have come too late—a day too late! Yesterday—last evening, Anthony asked me to marry him!"

"And you said ' yes ' ?" cries the other, rising too, forgetting for the moment her mincing airs and girl-gait, and speaking in a voice so shrill, genuine and resonant, that, did not the evidence of Joan's senses tell her that it proceeded from Mrs. Wolferstan's mouth, she would have disbelieved in the possibility of its being hers. "*And you said yes?*"

"I said ' yes.' Is there any reason why I should not say ' yes' ?"

They stand facing each other; Joan tall and pale, and resolute; her two hands straitly clasped together, and her courage gathered up; for is not this the brunt of the battle?

"What!" cries the elder woman, her voice rising to the neighbourhood of a scream, and for an instant forgetting even her complexion as she pushes up her veil, as if to get air at any price, even at the price of exposing her face—painted, gummed, and stuck together as it is—to the gaze of the pitiless western sun, and of Joan's steady eyes. "What!—you can stand there and look me, his mother, in the face and ask, 'is there any reason why you should not marry my son!'—you, too, whom I credited with such sound sense!"— (whimpering off into fatuity again).

"Are you going to tell me that a marriage with me must be a disadvantageous one for any man, much more for one who, like your son, might ask and get so much?" says Joan, speaking in a low voice, but quite calmly and gently. "I know it! I quite agree with you! —Are you going to tell me that I am poor— almost destitute—that I have very undesirable relations—that I have sunk to a grade in society far below your or my own natural level? It is all quite true! I quite agree with you; but—" (her voice rising a little, and a happy moisture tempering the fire of her brave blue eyes) "but he knows it all too, and he has overlooked it!"

"I protest that I am quite unable to follow you!" says Mrs. Wolferstan coldly. She has sat down again as if exhausted—sat down

with a sudden confidence, which shows her to
be no *habitué* of the Moberley chairs; has
pulled down her veil again, and resumed her
chilly every day voice: "I never was so
mistaken in any one in my life—I, who
generally am supposed to have a good deal of
insight into character!—you affect to be
alluding to the draw-backs that there are to
a union with you, and you pass over in total
silence, the one insuperable objection; in
comparison of which, all the others are trifles
light as air—as air!" (fretfully waving about
a large black fan).

"What do you mean?" asks Joan slowly;
her blue eyes widening in a painful wonder:
"as God lives, I have told you all the draw-
backs to myself that I know of: certainly
they are many and great enough: I blame
no mother for giving me a cold welcome, but
you hint at something else—something worse!
—what else can there be? known to you, unknown to me?"

"How!" cries the other in accents of

unfeigned amazement and dismay; "are you serious? but indeed there is no appearance of insincerity about you; is it possible that you do not know the—really it is difficult to know how to word it—the deplorable—the lamentable circumstances?"

"I know nothing!" answers Joan; her composure breaking a little, and speaking in quick and shaken tones; "I am in the dark! I see—" (lifting up her hands, as if to ward off a blow about to fall)—"I see that something dreadful is coming; if you have any mercy—if you have any humanity—let it come quickly!"

"Is it possible?" says the other, in a scared voice; "who could have imagined such a thing? is it possible that you are ignorant—that you have not heard—that no one has ever told you about—about—*your father?*"

"My father! I know absolutely nothing of him! I have vaguely heard that he was rather wild, and that he died when I was ten months old; is there anything to hear? anything bad ?" (her voice sinking to a suffocated whisper).

All the blood has, in a moment, drained itself away from her sweet cheeks; even from the lips, but now so ripely dewily red : all the colour that is left in her centres in her eyes, that—wide and blue and dimly frightened—stare out from her small white face.

"This is too shocking !" cries Mrs. Wolferstan, rising hastily, and making for the door ; "you must excuse me, I will leave you !—I must go home !—I will write ;—you may depend upon me ; as soon as I reach home I will write !"

"You will not write !" says Joan, rapidly crossing the room ; standing with her back against the door, and speaking in low stern tones, steadied by an enormous effort—"you will tell me—tell me now—before you leave this room !"

"It is absolutely impossible !" says Mrs. Wolferstan, whimpering, and feeling with futile fingers for the useless door-handle. "I

never was able to break anything to anybody
in my life ! I never had the nerve for it ; I
refer you to your aunt ; she knows the whole
affair ; she will tell you."

" *You* will tell me !" repeats Joan, still in
the same resolute low voice, as she stands—
inexorable guardian—with her straight young
back against the door panel. No long-buried
god or marble nymph was ever so pale as
she ; nor did ever blue eyes look out in frozen
terror from a more ashy face. "You will
tell me ; you have begun, and you must end ;
if I can bear to hear, you can bear to speak !"

" I never was placed in such a position in
my life !" says the elder woman, trembling
all over, and aimlessly fumbling for her
smelling bottle ; " I, too, who have always—
all my life been physically incapable of giving
pain to anyone ! I, who never could bear to
see a fly killed—but—since you insist upon
it—since you use compulsion—since you give
me no choice—I suppose I must be driven
—though certainly no one in the world is less

fitted for the task than I—to tell you that—
that—your father——"

She stops.

" Go on."

" That your father—really it is barbarous
to have to say such things of a parent to a
child—that your father, after having been
the scapegrace and *bête noire* of his family
all his life—after having nearly broken his
father's heart, and run through all his mother's
fortune, into which he came at his majority—
after having put himself entirely out of his
own station in society by contracting a
mésalliance with a barrack master's daughter
—you must excuse my saying so, but it was
what his family called it—put a climax to his
—his—misfortunes by——"

Again she stops, dead short, gasping.

" Go on !"

" By—by—well, it is not my fault—you
will have it—by forging his employer's signa-
ture—he had been taken into the employ of
a provincial banker as clerk—to a cheque

for a large amount. Out of regard to the
family, and especially out of regard to your
grandfather, whom all the world reverenced,
the banker abstained from prosecuting, and, I
am told, honestly tried to hush up the matter.
But you know," (with a shrug), "how impossible it is to keep these kind of things
quiet. In a day the affair had got wind, in a
week the whole country side, high and low,
gentle and simple, knew it. Soon afterwards, fortunately—one may really say, pro-
videntially—your father died. There, I hope
you are satisfied now!" sinking down on a
chair, and breaking, behind her swaddling
veil, into a torrent of feeble tears.

There is a silence, a dead icy silence ; at
least in the room ; for outside God's good air
is full of merry noises—the holiday shrieks
of the scampering Campidoglio children, the
triumphant clucking of the Sardanapalus
hens. After a while :

"What," says Joan, in a rough slow
whisper; reeling as one drunk, while her

haggard eyes roll round the miserable finery
of the little garish room ; " what—is—this—
you—have been saying ?   There—is—something—wrong—about my ears !   I—hear
wrong." Another pause. " What," her voice
rising with sudden leap into an anguished
loudness, as, staggering forwards, she con-
vulsively clutches the wrists of the cowering
old woman, while her wild eyes turn the full
agony of their blaze on her face ; " What ! do
you know who it is that you are speaking to ?
Do you know that it is I—Joan Dering—
whom you have been telling that her father was
a *forger*? that it was only by accident that he
did not die in a felon's gaol ?   You have lost
your wits, I say !—you have lost your wits !"
spasmodically shaking the frightened hands
that she holds.

" I have done nothing of the kind !" says
Mrs. Wolferstan, thoroughly alarmed and
sobbing angrily ; " let me go ! you have no
right to be so violent !   I have not said one
word for the truth of which I cannot vouch.

I am hardly likely to be inventive on such a subject; ask your aunt—ask anybody."

The sound of her peevish tremulous voice seems to bring Joan back to sanity. Slowly she looses her hands, and totters blindly back against the wall.

" It is true then!" she says, under her breath. " True—true—true !" repeating the word over several times, as if it were one of unfamiliar sound and strange meaning.

There is another lead-footed silence. Mrs. Wolferstan is ruefully regarding her wrists, on which Joan's agonised grasp has left distinct red marks. Joan herself is still leant against the wall, which, alone, seems to prevent her falling ; her hands clenched together in icy wedlock, her eyes stiffly fixed ; her red mouth pinched and pale, her dimples murdered and dead. Then she speaks in a harsh marred voice, with gaps between the broken words :

" They knew it, then, all along—all these years the people at Dering knew it !—among whom I held my head so high and lorded it over them because they were not so purely born as I! They knew it, and they did not taunt me with it—did not throw it in my teeth. Great God! they were forbearing!" lifting arms and clasped hands high above her head, and then letting them despairingly drop again.

" I suppose that they thought it kinder to keep you in the dark," says Mrs. Wolferstan querulously; for the tears she has shed have taken all the gum out of her eyelashes, and sent smeary runlets down her parti-coloured cheeks; " though, for my part, I think they were extremely ill-judged !"

" Kinder! kinder! kinder!" cries the girl, with a wild laugh, her voice at each word scaling new heights of woe. " Do you call that kind ? If they had been kind, they would have taught me, as soon as I could speak, that I was not like other children; that I had no right to play with them, or have hopes or a future like theirs. As soon as I could understand anything they should have told me that God had sent me into the world branded—*branded* to my life's end."

At the last words she falls forward on her trembling knees before a chair, and her stricken head sinks heavily on the gaudy faded worsted seat. There she lies, absolutely motionless, without a moan or a cry; only now and then a short dry sob tells that she still lives: that her aching soul is still held in the prison of her sweet white body. Outside still go on the gay every-day noises: the quick feet and high loud voices of the glad children; the emulous crowing of two rival cocks, each resolute to have the last word.

"I never was placed in such a position in my life," says Mrs. Wolferstan, beginning to sob again, and helplessly eyeing her prone companion. "I, too, to whom the sight of suffering has always been unendurable; I remember when I was a child, when my canary died—I think the cat killed it—I cried without stopping for three whole days; they could not pacify me. I said, 'Leave me alone, I will die too.' I recollect it as if it were yesterday."

Her foolish words knock at the door of Joan's brain without gaining any admittance. They convey no more meaning to her mind than does the talk of the loud evening rooks to us. After an interval—a long, long interval, neither of them ever knows how long—Joan slowly lifts her face—a face unswollen, undiscoloured by any tears, for tears that come hurrying at the call of any surface butterfly sorrow hold cruelly aloof from a master grief;—a face across which is for ever written the superscription of an unutterable woe. Then she speaks in a collected even voice, no longer hoarse or distraught.

"When you first came here to-day," she says, addressing Mrs. Wolferstan, and holding her by the solemnity of her great and woful eyes, "you told me that when you had explained yourself I should agree with you.

You are right; I do agree with you." No answer. Another heavy silence. "You came," says Joan slowly, still in the same composed tone, with not even a gasp or catching of the breath, "to rescue your son from the infamy of marrying a forger's daughter. Well, you have succeeded—he is safe. And now, will you go, please? I think I should be glad if you would go."

Mastered by the silent tragedy of her eyes, the other turns without a word and moves limp and crest-fallen to the door, but before she can turn the door-handle Joan is again beside her.

"I was wrong," she says; "discourteous; I ask your pardon. If I had been in your place I should have done as you have done; probably I should have done it more harshly, for in the face of such a peril one could not be scrupulous, or pick one's words. I bear you no malice. Good-bye."

As she speaks she puts out an ice-cold hand, and the other taking it, silently goes.

CHAPTER XXVIII.

HE day that has been so fair and brave, is waning. The gray-wimpled night steps on. The rival cocks have each led their separate file of wives, daughters, and cousins, to the privacy of the hen-house perch, where already slumbering with sunk necks, drooped tails, and pouted busts, they ante-date the coming night. The Campidoglio children still shriek and plunge and ravage, with all the terrible vivacity of youth.

The hour draws nigh when Wolferstan and his love are again to meet, for sweet good-

night speech by the twilight waves. It was
only by this concession that she escaped in
the morning from his grudging eyes and de-
taining arms. For a quarter of an hour he
has been trudging impatiently up and down
on the soft loose sand and sour small grass of
the dunes, his quick look turned sometimes
seawards, but oftener towards the inland
landscape, where, in the utter mellow stillness of even, spread the shaven corn-fields,
the steamy meadows, the red cottage roofs,
and heavy-weighted apple orchards.

To his hurrying thought, his love's steps
seem tardy. Each moment that she delays
is so much coin filched from their treasury.
What right has she thus to fritter the golden
sands of their love time ? As he so chidingly
thinks, there becomes visible to his intent eyes
a figure, small and indistinct from distance,
outlined against the pallid primrose of the
sky. It is she at last. His first impulse is
to go hastily to meet her, but a superstitious
feeling restrains him.

" I will not go to her : she shall come to me ; we will meet on the same spot where we met this morning : it will be a good omen."

So he stands still and watches her. She seems to him to come but slowly ; and her feet, being such light ones, and having so slender a body to upbear, trail but heavily after each other. But she is close to him now : she, who, five minutes ago, was a dim little blur—a blur that might turn out to be a cow, or a sheep, or even one of the Sardanapalus pigs, is now seen to be a wonderful fair woman, of high stature and grave countenance, in a black gown. He had meant to have reproached her ; but, as he looks upon her, his reproaches die away in utter joy and pride. Dumbly he holds out his arms to her. Dumbly too, she comes up to him ; and, without any bidding, lays her soft arms about his neck ; and lifting her face to his, says, in a clear plain voice, " Kiss me."

As she speaks, no red love-wave—no rosy

torrent of virgin shame sweeps across her
cheeks: her eyelids do not quiver, nor her
eyes droop. Wolferstan is not the man to
need that such an invitation should be twice
repeated. Profoundly astonished (though not
even to himself would he own this), and still
more profoundly glad, he snatches her to his
hurrying heart. After awhile she withdraws
herself somewhat from him, and still holding
up a face, whose whiteness not even all his
many kisses have been able to dye with any
vermeil stain, she says in a calm slow voice:

"You are surprised at me!—you wonder
what has made me suddenly so forward!—
ah!" (with a long sigh), "one does not stand
much on forms when one is saying 'good-
bye'!"

"Good-bye?" he cries startled, then, quickly
recovering his happy confidence—"ah! you
mean 'God be with you!' I hope he will;
now that you are beside me, he is more likely
to be."

"Nay," she answers, looking at him with

a solemn tenderness; " I mean 'good-bye'
— 'farewell' — whatever other word most
means leave-taking !"

" Leave-taking !" he echoes, alarmed and
puzzled ; " why should we speak of leave-
taking ?—are you going anywhere ?"

" Ay !" she says, with a bitter smile ; " I
am going away from hope and love and
pleasantness ! I wish — oh, I wish that I
were going away from life too ! but that is
not likely !—at twenty, that is not likely !"

"Joan !" he says, now thoroughly frightened,
while a vague cold terror girdles his heart and
chills the hot river in his young veins ; " Joan !
what are you saying ? I know that there can
be nothing amiss really—what could there be ?
—what could have happened within these few
hours ?"

" Nothing has happened !" she answers, her
pale lips still curving in that most bitter smile ;
" only that to-day I have been my own sexton
and have been burying my past and my future
together in one deep grave ; oh love !" (in a

voice, anguished indeed, but more natural—
more like herself than her late so icy composure), "your labour is lost! you need not
try to hide it from me any more; I know—
to-day I know—what I am! your mother has
told me!"

"What!" he cries, his face, a moment ago
goodly and content as the fleckless sky above
him, or the meek summer sea at his feet, all
overcast with sudden clouds, while his eyes
dart steely shafts of anger and fear; "what!
she has dared!——"

"Hush!" she says with low authority, laying her cold hand on his wrathful mouth;
"hush! She did well! Had I been she,
and she I, I should have done the same. I
am glad—" (speaking with firm and weighty
slowness), "yes, glad that I have learned in
time what an injury I was going to do you:
I think—" (the solemnity of her tone tem-
pered by a great softness), "I think that you
know that I would not willingly do you a
mischief!"

"I am glad of it," he says quickly. "God grant that we mean the same thing! There is only one real mischief that you could do me!"

"And you knew it all along—all the time!" she cries—a sort of triumph in her voice, "and yet you would have kept silence all your life, and have set me at your side as your honoured wife! Oh, love, it was well and worthily done of you, and I thank you—from the bottom of my heart I thank you for it!"

As she speaks, she humbly takes his hand and kisses it, while the tears, so long in coming, shower at last, in plentiful salt rain from her parched eyes.

"For God's sake, stop!" cries Anthony, snatching away his hand; "you humiliate me! Why, pray!" he goes on, red and stammering, "why should I have told you about it? why should we waste time in speaking of so ugly and outworn, and—and

—unimportant a subject ?   Have not we had
pleasanter themes, Joan ?"

She shakes her head sadly. " Unimportant, is it ?   Alas ! it is important enough to
set us two for ever asunder !"

" What !" he says, falling back uncertainly
a step or two, as if one had heavily and suddenly struck him, while a great dread slides
coldly along his limbs, and chokes back the
crowding words that are hurrying to his lips.

" Do you think," she says, speaking with
the greatest sweetness, yet resolution withal,
" that I love you so poorly as to saddle you
for ever with my disgrace ?   Do you think
that I will let you—willing as you are—God
bless you for that willingness !—couple your
good clean name with my stained one ?"

" How !" he cries ; the laggard words
coming quickly enough now, in torrent flow ;
words of utter scorn and contempt ; " do I
understand you right ?   Is it my rational,
sweet, sensible Joan that is speaking ?   Are
you going to set up a phantom, a bogy be-

tween us ?—because there are no real hin-
drances—because the path that leads from me
to you is smooth and level as path can be ;
must you yourself build up impediments and
throw obstacles ? — impediments of straw—
obstacles of air !"

She is silent. Her wet eyes have travelled
away to the red western wave, which seems
to be dyed with the blood of all the roses that
have blossomed since the world was.

" It makes my blood boil to hear you talk
of your stained name !" he says feverishly,
beginning restlessly to walk up and down on
the little hillock ; " how can any stain come
near my unsullied lily ?—and that name,"—
(stopping beside her, and speaking with the
utmost eagerness) — " and that name !—not
much longer will it be yours ! Soon, very
soon, mine, which you praise for its clean-
ness, will be yours too ; will not it, beloved ?
will not it ?"

" Never !" she says, looking solemnly and
proudly up to heaven's vault darkening over

their heads. "I shall never bear your or any other man's name; into no man's home will I carry my disgrace."

"You are consistent!" says the young man bitterly; "in one breath you tell me that you will never willingly do me a mischief; and in the next you threaten me with what you know will put out my sun and darken my day!"

"Not darken it!" she says gently. "God forbid!—perhaps for a little while I may sadden it; but in that I do you no unkindness; we are none of us the worse for being a little sad sometimes. Oh, my love!" (breaking into a most tender, rueful, drowning smile) "my comely love! you are so good and goodly; your life is so rich in all pleasant things that you cannot fret long; it would be unnatural that you should, because one pleasant thing—such a poor and paltry one too—is taken from you!"

"It is not taken from me!" he cries in a rough loud voice, up-gathering her into his strong embrace; "do not dare to say so!

As easily can your small fingers unwind my arms from about you—let them try!—so easily can you unwind your life from mine !—they are twisted together warp and woof! Only God—only God, I say, has leave to give and again take back His gifts, none blaming Him!"

She is dumb. Silently weeping, she lies in the gaol of her one love's vigorous arms; in no hurry, perhaps, to escape from that embrace, so soon to be for ever foregone. And he knows that he might as well have spoken to the deaf tides, or the glooming sands. With a sudden revulsion of feeling—in a transport of resentment and sharp pain he lets her go ; looses her so suddenly, that at first she staggers as one about to fall.

" Go !" he says rudely ; while through the dusk of the hastening night his eyes dart their angry bright ray into hers ; "go !— I set you free !—practise your cheap fortitude ! complete the renunciation that costs you so little ! If you are as pure as snow, you are also as cold. Go !"

" Am I cold ?" she says, in a low and broken voice, though she lifts her fair head spiritedly and her eyes meet his—meek, yet unflinching ; " if, to reckon up how many hours the different moments and half-hours of our meetings make up, and to count them alone as the grain of life, and all else but the chaff—if that is to be cold—well, yes—then I am cold, and you do well to call me so."

Her limbs are trembling so much that they feel as if they would give way beneath her ; so she sits down on the dry barren hill, and he throws himself on the ground beside her. There is a long, long silence ; while they two sit wordlessly looking out on the sea and listening to its pauseless song. The sea is a singer that never needs to stop and take breath. The sun is dead, and the waves have forgotten him—forgotten him as utterly as if he had never laid his royal head on their breast. They are paying their homage now to the lady moon, who, kirtled with lawny clouds, is beginning to float up the sky. She is only a half-moon : no great round yellow harvest orb; and yet beneath her a field of pale lustre spreads over the sea; one broad white sail on the horizon has caught her light and glimmers with uncertain silver. Joan's head has sunk on her love's shoulder : their hands are closely locked together. He is the first to speak.

"Joan!" he says, in a whisper of passionate persuasion, so low as to be hardly audible above the ocean's quiet plain song; "Joan! will you stay with me? tell me that you will! tell me that I have prevailed!"

She sighs heavily.

"Love!" she says, in a deprecating voice, timorous yet resolved; "do not thrust me from you as you did just now; but, indeed, I can never be your wife; if I were, I should have no content or comfort of my life for thinking what a wrong and a discredit I had done you! oh, beloved—do not be angry with me—but you know that to not many of us is given a great stability of will or purpose; what

we wish to-day, often we unwish to-morrow :
or if not to-morrow—to-morrow five years—
to-morrow ten years — to-morrow twenty
years—and whether it came soon or came
late, always I should have upon me the heavy
fear that a day might dawn when you would
repent of the sacrifice you had made—when
you would wish it again unmade, and when
it would be too late to unmake it !"

He does not answer. The pale moon is
shining on his pale face, and coldly pointing
out its discomfiture.

"I see," she says, looking up to heaven
with a solemn steadfastness; "that God
destines me for a lonely life; oh, my darling !
do not be sorry for me for that; to-night
indeed" (sobbing quietly), "I think that I
am as miserable as any woman can be, but
even now I can look on ahead and see a life
when I shall not be miserable—a life full of
work to do and people to love; and if, by and
by, now and again, I hear of you as good
and prosperous—prosperous in soul and in the

higher life as well as in earthly well-being, then—then—though I am alone, I shall not be unhappy — certainly I shall not be un-happy!"

He has buried his face on her knees that she may not see the tears that disfigure it. She passes her light hand fondly over the smooth brown hair that the night dews are already beginning to wet. The moon has risen higher. One can dimly see the long cold rippling smiles curve the cheek of the great water, and the snow-crests of the little waves shine whitely in turning over on the dark beach.

"And if," says Joan weeping, though her eyes shine with a confident clear light; "and if you are still resolute to love me—if death finds us still remembering each other, then who will dare to say that hereafter we may not belong to each other in some other world, where the sins of the fathers are not visited on the children; Anthony, good-bye! bid me God speed as I bid you!—I must go!"

He has lifted his face from her lap : the face
that is wont to be so debonnair, so curved with
young laughter, so lit up by joy. Marred
and wan, you would hardly know it to be
Anthony's.

"Go ?" he says, in an unsteady voice ;
" already ?"

" Already !" she answers, still weeping ;
" it must be done, so it had best be done
quickly ; oh, my one love !" (girdling him for
the last time with her fair arms, and closely
pressing him to her innocent breast), " you
have been very good and tender to me, and I
would have been good and tender to you too ;
we would have outdone each other in kindness
and love ; God keep you, Anthony !—though
henceforth our roads lie apart, I pray—oh,
pray you too—that perhaps they may meet
at the end !"

" They will meet before the end !" he cries,
in a passionate loud voice ; "say what you
will—do what you will—we have not yet
done with each other ; time that wastes and

crumbles everything, will waste and crumble your resolve—lovely and loving as you are, do you think that you will be able to bear the barren desert doom that you destine for yourself? it is impossible, monstrous, out of nature! yet—yet" (his voice taking a note of almost triumphant exultation), "yet—yet—you will come to me!—yet—yet again my arms will hold your beloved sweet body! you will come to me I tell you! and, be it soon or be it late, I shall be ready—I shall be waiting!"

"Will you?" she says, shaking her head sorrowfully with a sweet wet smile; "I think not—I think that you will grow tired before I shall! nay, love! till God who makes all things clean, shall wipe away the stain from me, we two shall meet in love and fellowship never again!"

CHAPTER XXIX.

HE Moberley tea has long been spread. The cold resurrection pie —the one viand on the earth's face more abominable than hot resurrection pie— already adorns the board, when Joan very softly opens the hall door, in the hope that, by an exceedingly cautious entry, she may succeed in slipping upstairs unseen, unheard, unquestioned. But in this vain hope she is deceived ; for no sooner does the slight click that the latch gives in being lifted make itself heard, than the drawing-room door, which has apparently been purposely left ajar, opens suddenly, and in the aperture appears the form of Mrs. Moberley, while over her bounteous shoulders is seen a perspective of younger faces, Bell's and Diana's.

"Why, bless me, child, where have you been?" cries the elder lady, in a tone of mixed anger and relieved anxiety; "I was just going to send out Sarah with a lanthorn to look for you. Do you know what time it is?"

The light in the passage is fortunately but dim. Joan's head is bent, her hat is tilted over her eyes.

"I was sitting by the sea," she says faintly. "You know I love the sea."

"The sea, indeed!" retorts Mrs. Moberley, in a scolding and somewhat incredulous tone. "I think the sea has a broad back. To tell you the truth, young lady, I think you are far too fond of *stravaguing* about by yourself at odd hours, when you know quite well, too, that you need never go out alone; it is but a poor compliment to your cousins, and I am sure I do not know when either of them has ever refused to give you her company."

" I am sorry," answers Joan, bending her head—damp with the soft night dews—still lower on her breast, and speaking in a small submissive voice.

" I must say"—chimes in Bell, following one of the most unamiable rules that guide human nature's often unamiable actions, and giving a prod with her bayonet, too, to the fallen—" I must say, Joan, that it was very shabby of you slipping out without giving any of us the least hint of what Mrs. Wolferstan came about after all. Come, now, we may as well hear now, at all events; or, perhaps"—(with a huffy laugh)—" perhaps it is a secret, and I have no business to ask."

Joan's white face takes a faint tinge of uneasy red at this question; though, perhaps, the one jet of dim ill-smelling gas does not betray her; while, with infinite difficulty, she searches among her word-stores for an answer that shall be evasive, probable, and conciliating. But it is so long in coming, that Arabella has time to speak again.

"It was a pity," she says sarcastically, "that you did not warn Mrs. Wolferstan how thin these walls are; if you had, I think she would not have raised her voice so high. We heard her several times so loud, did not we, mother? did not we, Di? We thought that you must be having a regular quarrel."

"Did you?" says Joan, indistinctly, and catching her breath a little, as she leans heavily against the grimy marbled paper of the passage wall.

"Dear me!" says Mrs. Moberley, recovering her good humour, which, indeed, she seldom mislays for long, and shaking her head meditatively, "dear me! what a thing dress is, to be sure! she must be my age if she is a day! She was married to old Wolferstan a good twelvemonth before Moberley offered to me, and yet, to-day to see her back and the jaunty way she skipped into

the carriage, you might have taken her for
sixteen."

"If her back looks sixteen," says Diana,
trenchantly, "her face looks a hundred. For
my part, I had rather strike a balance, and
look fifty all over like you, mother!"

"Think of me in a sprigged frock and a
flyaway hat like that!" cries Mrs. Moberley,
a fat laugh agitating her whole person like a
dish of jelly too quickly carried; "I should
do to frighten the crows. Come along, girls;
if the tea is not drawn now it never will be,
for it has been standing the best part of an
hour."

And thus prosaically, with over-drawn tea
and resurrection pie, closes the most tragic
day of Joan's hitherto history. There are
many tragedies that are acted in dumb show;
none but the actors guessing at all that they
are being played; and there are many others
that are clad in very homely and fustian
clothes. There are two facts in human
history—two, at first sight, contradictory

propositions — that I think surprise me equally, viz., the ease with which we sometimes die; and the difficulty that there sometimes is in killing us. Often a pin prick lets out our souls. Often again, we are cut in two, as it were, like a worm or a snake, and yet manage to wriggle ourselves together again. As the days go on, Joan wonders at her own vitality.

Between one sunrise and one moonrise, in a space shorter than the life of a gnat or a convolvulus, she has seen her past and her future pass away hand in hand to a death which holds out no dimmest hope of a resurrection. And yet she falls down senseless, in no sudden syncope. She has no brain fever. Neither her clear wits nor her even-pulsing health suffer any hurt or eclipse. When the cracked bell rings to dinner, she eats. When bed-time comes, she sleeps. When Mrs. Moberley's caps pass the boundary of moderate dilapidation, she makes her new ones. Sometimes she laughs. It is mostly the dogs who make her laugh. In her human surroundings, she does not find much to stir her rare and tardy merriment; but she has always a smile for Mr. Brown, and mostly one for Regy and Algy. Perhaps the very circumstance which, at the time, seems to put the crown upon her grief and discomfort; viz., the stringent necessity for hiding her sorrow from the curious prying Moberley eyes;—stringent indeed, for, if it is known to the Moberleys, then it is also known to Micky; if to Micky, then also to the whole barracks; if to all the barracks, then to all Helmsley too;—the necessity for concealing her tears, nay, altogether suppressing them for fear of the traces they leave, is after all, the best thing that could have happened to her. Perhaps the strain that she has to put upon herself—the obligation to eat when she is not hungry, to laugh when she is not mirthful, to talk when her tongue cleaves to the roof of her mouth—saves her from that collapse which sometimes follows an indulged grief.

But she suffers! oh she suffers! Her indigent room and meagre truckle bed, her lame furniture and halt crockery can bear witness that she suffers. Often, kneeling in the dark—(a candle might betray her)—with face hard pressed against the miserable rush-bottomed seat of one of her two chairs, she hears the hospital clock toll the eerie hours of deepest night, while she, in wide-awake anguish, is wrestling with her trouble; wrestling with the sometimes nigh-conquering longing, to take back again the good she has foregone; to fulfil even thus early her love's prophecy, and say to him, " I come to you! you have prevailed!" to feel once again his lips married in closest wedlock to hers; to hear his joyous voice softly calling her by the small old-fashioned name that he has thought so fair, and sweet. But from all her contests she comes out dismally victorious. Daily the post goes out, and carries no message to the sweetheart she has dismissed.

"I must live in other people's happiness!" she cries to herself a hundred times a day; trying earnestly to brace her nerves and lift her heart to the level of that high, but cold and difficult destiny. But almost as often as she raises it, it falls back; down dragged by a most bitter human yearning for some warm own private bliss; some happiness that shines not only reflected from other faces, as the sun shines in water, or on burnished brass, but that shall be for warmth and glory and comfort, as the sun himself.

"Live in other people's happiness? How is that possible? As long as I have a mouth myself, will the food that is put into other mouths satisfy me? Will it content me that other women's arms enfold their lovers, though mine are empty?"

The one certain and tangible outcome of her pain is the resolve that every day strengthens, to have done, as soon as may be, with this life of dependence and inertia. Woman's work indeed—at least bread-win-

ning work—is not over plenty in this present
world ; neither is it ordinarily pleasant or
remunerative, or with much of hope or pro-
gress in it ; but it is work. In the energy of
work—good work, bad work, what work
you will—suffering is drowned. Never waste
your pity on the real workers of this life.
Harsh, unlovely, as their outward surroundings may apparently be ; yet they neither
ask for nor need your compassion. Who feels
his wounds in the stress and heat of the
fight ?

Never, since she entered Mrs. Moberley's
door, has Joan's determination to earn her
own bread faltered or failed ; she being ever of
too high and free a spirit to sit down con-
tentedly under the yoke of obligation and
sloth. What alone has delayed the hitherto
execution of her design is diffidence as to her
own competence for that special branch of
labour, towards which almost every educated
woman, to whom bread lacks, intuitively
turns, viz., teaching.

Her education, indeed—the wide fine cul-
ture, whose original intention was to ornament
and occupy the leisure of a luxurious and
wealthy life—has fitted her, more than most
girls are fitted, for the task she has set herself, and her persevering lessons to Diana
have given her, at least in some degree, the
faculty of teaching and the habit of patience.
The tool then is ready.   All that yet lacks is
the material to work upon.

Miss Dering's project meets with but small
favour in her family's eyes when she opens
her mind to them upon it.

"Please yourself, and you'll please me!"
says Mrs. Moberley in an offended tone;
using the formula of magnanimous sound but
contracted meaning, which she always employs
when anything has occurred to ruffle her;
"but I will say, Joan, that it is a sad take-
down for us all!   Not one of us has ever had
anything to do with teaching; and, say what
you please, it is no better than a kind of
upper servant, without any tips or perquisites

either. However, 'a wilful man will have his way,' and as soon as you are tired of your freak, you have nothing to do but dash into the train and come straight off here again! You will always find a knife and fork ready for you—always!"

They say that to all hands willing to labour work comes, but its coming is sometimes tardy. Though Joan's short and temperately worded advertisement has travelled off into every home where the *Times, Standard,* etc., make their way, yet, as the weeks go on, the postman's hands are not overladen with answers for her. No one seems very anxious to have Joan Dering to teach their progeny. For one person who slackly and faintly desires a governess, nine hundred and ninety-nine earnestly and prayerfully clamour for a cook.

Since the insertion of the advertisement she has received but six replies in all : five to be at once dismissed as absolutely undesirable and utterly inadmissible. The sixth is patently undesirable too ; but, being the last, Joan is loth quite to dismiss it. She has even braced her mind to close with its untempting offers, if nothing better turn up.

It is unjust, impossible, that she should keep Anthony for ever in banishment from his own home, and anything, any servitude, any petty tyranny, would be preferable to his returning to find her still here. While she is yet in this state of uncertainty and oscillation, one more calamity befalls her. Mr. Brown sickens—sickens of distemper—and languishes for many weeks, hovering between life and death.

Any one who has watched this terrible disease will know of how perilous, cruel, and wearing a nature it is to the sufferer; how disheartening—sometimes heartrending—to the human on-looker, powerless to assuage those so patiently borne dumb agonies. Through long days Joan sits beside Mr. Brown's sick basket, scarcely giving herself time for necessary food, rest or exercise.

Through many vigils she watches by him; giving him his beef-tea and his physic with as tender a punctuality as if he were her brother.

In painfully watching his ribs grow daily more prominent, his poor coat more staring, and his dear goggle eyes more pathetic, Joan goes nigh to forgetting for the moment (despise her as you will for it) that such a person as Wolferstan exists. Mr. Brown is certainly very ill, though never so ill as to be unable to shake hands; once or twice indeed, when he is at his worst, he gives the wrong paw—the left instead of the right—but, except for this trifling inaccuracy, he never forgets his accomplishment. As it is his only one, it is well that he should have a good firm grip of it.

By and by Joan's patient nursing gains its reward, for Mr. Brown lives. He is spared, we will hope, for many future years of usefulness; to bury and again exhume, many a bone, to insult many more dynasties of mysteriously exasperating butcher's boys, to have his ears boxed by many another spiteful tom-cat.   Mr. Brown lives, and Joan is very —very glad !

CHAPTER XXX.

IME, the strong scythesman, mows the days. After all, this is an outworn simile, and will soon be unintelligible. Scythes are walking quickly away into the limbo of the past and the outgrown; walking away after flails, spinning-wheels, and distaffs.

In a short time we shall be obliged, in our metaphors and allegories, to represent Time and Death, each with a steam mowing-machine. Oh, Watt! Watt! you and your tea-kettle have made sad havoc in the poetry of our daily life! The brave summer fire has burnt itself out to its last embers. The flower time is dead. The heavy-weighted purple fruit time is dead too. Between the death days of these sister seasons the space always seems short and soon spanned.

> " The squirrel's granary is full,
>   And the harvest done !"

The plums have fulfilled their annual vocation of making jam, and causing colics ; the apples lie perdu in tarts ; the morella cherries have drunk themselves to death in brandy bottles ; the hips and haws are quickly vanishing beneath the beaks of the little hungry finches ; and one recollects again that the holly—hard and prickly December beauty —exists. Earth has stripped off all her green ribbons, and her rainbow gauds, and has lain down to take her rest in her russet gown. Of all her choristers, there is only the bold cock-robin left to sing her to sleep. It is four months and a bit since Wolferstan went— since, weepingly, his love said to him, " God

keep you, Anthony!" Four months! It is
then time that she should be beginning to
forget him. Between us and the events of
four months ago, a film is mostly drawn; a
film, sometimes of a consistency no greater
than a gossamer; sometimes as substantial as
a stout cambric handkerchief.

"We slightly remember our felicities, and
the smartest strokes of affliction leave but
short smart upon us. Sense endureth no ex-
tremities, and sorrows destroy us or themselves."

Often we are inclined to pule and whimper
over the weakness of our memories, but who
would accept the other alternative? Who
would care to recollect, with the vividness
and accuracy with which he can recall the
incidents of yesterday, his birth, his Alex-
andra bottle, his first whipping? Portland
Villa, with the rest of the world, has taken
the shivering plunge into winter—shivering,
truly this year. Scourging winds, lashing
rains, marrow searching fogs, numbing frosts,

glaring snows! On all these instruments in turn winter plays his terrible marches and solemn fugues. He seems resolute to show in how infinite a variety of ways he can make himself feared and hated. But, indeed, who has ever doubted his dread ability?

" A hard winter !" say even they who dwell in solid houses with well-seasoned doors and nicely-fitting windows ; how much more then the inhabitants of a gimcrack one brick villa residence ? A villa residence too, by no means in the best repair ! with slates lacking from the roof : with dead-leaf-choked gutters and suffocated spouts. On Joan's walls great green patches of damp, like ugly plague spots, growths of furry mould, make their appearance. In the eerie winter nights the wind-giant takes the rotten casements in his Titan hands, and makes the whole flimsy house stagger and tremble. Under the warped door, through the chinks and gaps of the window-frames, comes the iced blast; and pierces to the bone the poor soul who, such a few months ago, was panting and gasping in this now frozen attic. Oh, if she could but have saved some of her then super-fluous warmth for these miserable winter nights!

The Abbey is empty. Since the exodus it made on one August day, the family has not returned. For the first time within the memory of man, it does not come down for Christmas; nor perform its wonted duty of Christmas-treeing and bran-pieing the children of the neighbourhood, dancing the adolescents and dining the adults.

It is Christmas day—a streaming pouring Christmas day, when earth and heaven fold each other in one gray embrace, and the horizon is bounded by the window-pane. The Moberley family have dauntlessly, with soaked boots and sludged petticoats, slipped and swum along the flooded road—half ice, half dreary thaw—to the Garrison church. They have listened to a sermon evidently originally written for a fine Christmas day, and, by some oversight, not adapted to the present circumstances—a sermon in which the clergyman directed their attention and admiration towards the glorious sunbeams streaming into the church, which, in point of fact, is so dark that the gas has to be lit.

They are at home again now; are also again dry, and have dined. For a wonder the butcher has not forgotten to bring the beef, nor is there lacking one of those puddings so unaccountably associated with Christ's birth. Mrs. Moberley even with desperate determination to make merry, insists on brewing a small bowl of punch, and proposes several dismal toasts. "The Queen!" "The Military!" etc. They are drunk in dejected silence.

"It is not in the least like Christmas!" she says for the twentieth time; "since the year that your papa died"—(glancing at Mr. Moberley's picture which Sarah, in a well-meant but ill-executed effort to be seasonable and festive, has smothered to the nose in

funeral yew)—"since the year that your
papa died, I never remember such a Christmas!—never!"

In the corner of her usually jovial eye,
there is a tear; whether due to her lost mate
or her present ennui is not known.

"And to think of this time last year!"
says Bell, beginning to cry; "just at this
hour we were thinking of going to dress for
the ball at the barracks, Bobby Butler's
bouquet had just come, and we were compar-
ing notes—do you recollect, Di?—as to which
was the choicest, his or Micky's!—mine had
more camellias—yours more stephanotis!—
and now!"—

Her sobs choke her.

"The Infirmary Ball indefinitely post-
poned!" says Diana, beginning tragically to
check off their misfortunes on her fingers;
"the Assembly utterly quashed! no talk of
anything at the barracks, and the Abbey shut
up! I declare I do not see what use there
is in going on living!"

Joan's leaden heart echoes this sentiment; though for widely different reasons. On what portion of her life dare she fix her eyes? She must keep them, if possible, glued to this narrow strip of barren present on which she stands. Against her will, her winged thoughts carry her back to that last gone Christmas Day, which seems to her now to be clothed in gold and pearl and crimson, like some opulent apocalyptic vision. As if it were some other Joan, she sees herself sitting as hostess in her great carved chair at the end of the long and dainty table: the bounteous red fire roaring and racing up the wide-throated chimney; the softly shining white tapers in old venetian chandelier, and polished brass sconces: the goodly throng of merry guests; the gay stir of talk; the bandied repartee; the thrust and parry of light wit. Let us at least thank whatever gods there be, that we are not allowed to see our own faces, in 'the future's dread looking-glass. But if the "was" is hard to

face, how much harder the "might have
been"—that radiant child that died at its
birth. By this time, she might have been
Wolferstan's wife. By this time the fever
and effervescence of lover-love might have
been lost and swallowed up in the wide calm
sea of wedded bliss.

She turns with a shudder from her own
lot—the annihilated past, the numb present,
the ink-coloured future! But though her
own life-garden be laid waste; though its
flowers be dead and its sweet buds trampled
and gone—yet is this any reason why, by
her gloom, she should make yet more dull
and stale the narrow lives around her?

"You despair too soon!" she says, with a
smile, whose neighbourhood to tears they
are both too preoccupied and too dull-
sighted to perceive; "you do not know from
what unlooked-for quarter something may
spring up for you! How little you expected
the yeomanry dance!"

Mrs. Moberley shakes her head. " I am

not a grumbler!" she says, speaking with slow emphasis; "I take the fat with the lean; but this I will say, that, happen what may, no bit of luck—no windfall, or legacy, or anything else, ever comes our way; if there were to be a rain of gold on all the country round to-morrow, it is my belief that it would leave us as dry as Gideon's fleece!"

Against so resolved a melancholy as this, who can strive? Joan desists from the attempt and goes with the stream. This dejection lasts with a few intervals of a more sanguine character throughout Christmas week; nor is the weather of a nature to disperse it. The old year weeps itself away. It is New Year's Day now. The new year has come in with no flourish of yellow sunbeams; no loud trumpeting of herald winds; no ermine mantle of snow. It has crept in noiseless and sullen, as if it were ashamed of itself. Even if there had been any sunshine to-day, it would by this time have been gone; for the short winter's day has closed in. That hour has come, which, in summer seems almost at the beginning of the day; in winter, at the end.

It is towards five o'clock. The curtains in the Moberley drawing-room are drawn together as closely as insufficient stuff and rings that decline to run will allow. Neither lamp nor candle is lit, and up the chimney climbs a merry well-fed fire, that sends long shadows up wall and ceiling. It must be a very ugly room indeed, that can look ugly when lighted by a cheerful fire, and a cheerful fire alone.

We all have our *beaux jours;* and the drawing-room at Portland Villa is looking almost pretty, thanks to being only half seen. On the floor, beside Mr. Brown's basket, Joan is sitting. He has insisted on shaking hands no less than twelve times running, and, thanks to his convalescent state, has been indulged in this unnecessarily often repeated salutation. Bell is hanging over a chair-back, which she is idly tilting, and is address-

ing him as " My ownest wuffy wuffy," a remark which he is treating with the silent
contempt that so foolish an apostrophe de-
serves. The door opens, and a head (for a
wonder not Sarah's) is put in. With one
leap the dogs bound from sleep into bark.
Even Mr. Brown staggers on to his shaky
legs, and contributes his feeble mite of ana-
thema.

" Any admission except on business ?" asks
a noisily merry man's voice. " May I be
allowed to announce myself, as Sarah does
not seem inclined to do so ?"

It is Mr. Brand.

" You are quite a stranger," cries Mrs.
Moberley, holding out both hands to her
warmly welcome guest. " Bell, poke the
fire. You see we are having blind man's
holiday ; but, indeed, you find us all sad in-
valids ; we caught shocking colds on Christ-
mas-day. Bell's has gone to her face"—(and,
indeed, to a close observer, Miss Moberley's
countenance does present a rhomboid or gib-

bous appearance)—" Diana's to her throat.
The night before last we·were quite frightened, she could scarce swallow; mine to my
chest—bark! bark! bark! it tears me to
pieces! Joan is the only one of us that is
hale and sound—nothing ails Joan!"

"Nothing ails Miss Joan, eh?" says Mr.
Brand, glancing down at the little regal head;
up and down whose burnished hair the red
fire-gleams are at merry play; at the long
lily neck, meek yet proud, too; at the large
white eyelids, so obstinately drooped; and
speaking in that tone of confident jocosity
which he never dares employ when *tête-à-tête*
with Miss Dering; but which he mostly uses
when backed by the support and presence of
the Moberley family. "Nothing ails Miss
Joan, eh?—that is well!"

Joan makes no sort of rejoinder. She
never answers Mr. Brand unless he puts a
point-blank question to her; and even then,
she seldom spares him anything larger than a
" yes" or a " no."

"You are as welcome as flowers in May," cries Mrs. Moberley, whose voice has already regained three-fourths of its normal joviality. "Regy! Algy! Charlie! I am ashamed of you! make room, sirs, make room! And if you have brought us a bit of news, you are welcomer still! We are famished for news."

"Well, I am glad to be able for once in my life to oblige you," replies Micky, with complacent familiarity, holding his broad fingers to the blaze and chafing them; "for, as it happens, I have a piece of news—a large new piece."

"Not really?"

"You are not joking?"

"What is it?" in three separate but simultaneous volleys.

"Ah, that is telling!" answers Micky, with a tantalizing school-boy laugh; "you must guess."

"I hope it is not any stupid public news!" says Bell, suspiciously; "nothing about the

Ministry or the Budget, or anything tiresome of that kind ; I do not call that news."

" It is not public news."

" Is it about anybody we know?" asks Diana, her fears taking a slightly different direction from her sister's.

" It is about somebody whom we all know —even Miss Joan," with a rather vindictive look at the silent figure, which has not changed its posture by a hair's breadth, or— beyond a cold hand shake—shown any con- sciousness of his presence.

" Bobby Butler has exchanged?"

" Jackson has got his step?"

"Or is going to be married?" suggests Mrs. Moberley, with a jolly laugh. " I do love to hear of a marriage ! After all," (with a sigh) " it is much the happiest state !"

" Go to the top of the class," cries Micky facetiously ; "you are nearest the mark ! It is a marriage, but it is not Jackson! it is not" (looking re-assuringly round on the girls)— " it is not any of us !"

"Not any of you?" echoes Bell, in a tone of mixed relief and disappointment; for if Mr. Brand has thus taken all potential sting out of his intelligence, he has also robbed it of its strongest element of excitement. "It is about some one who thinks himself a very much greater man than any of *us!*" continues Micky, with a rather spiteful intonation. "I should be sorry to buy him at his own valuation, and sell him at mine. There! I have given you a lead now!"

"Not Wolferstan!" "Not Anthony!" "Not the Colonel!" cry the three women, starting suddenly upright in their chairs, with wide eyes and panting breasts.

Mr. Brand nods. "Right you are! it is Wolferstan."

There is an awed silence. Mrs. Moberley is the first to break it.

"Caught at last!" she says, shaking her head several times, and speaking with a pensive accent. "Well, well! I should not wonder if he left a good many sore hearts behind him. Bonny fellow! he was not given those grey eyes for nothing."

"And who is the lady?" asks Bell, with a large sigh; "somebody high, no doubt?—a member of the peerage, I should not wonder!"

"Nothing of the kind!" replies the young man, brusquely; "a plain 'Miss,' like anybody else. I know nothing of her,"—(in a somewhat hold-cheap voice) — "no more, I should fancy, do you; though they say that she was staying at the Abbey in the autumn; possibly you may have seen her drive by. *Beauchamp*—or some such name."

"Seen her drive by, indeed!" cries Bell, magnificently tossing her mane; "why of course we know her! I should think we did — of course we have met at the Abbey."

"She was there the only time we ever dined there," puts in Diana hastily; "but she never spoke to, or took the least notice of us."

Joan is the only one of the party whom Mr. Brand's information has apparently not galvanized. At his news—(though certainly it must be news to her too)—no smallest exclamation passes her lips. When he spoke she was stroking Mr. Brown. She is stroking him still. Her little white hand is passing slowly down his back from his neck, along his tawny coat to his tail, and so again. The only difference is, that then it was a conscious action; now it is an absolutely unconscious one.

What a long way off these people's voices sound! Surely Micky's laugh must be in the next county, at least! Are they dreadful dream-people? Is this a dream-dog that is licking her fingers?

" It is quite an old affair, I am told," pursues Mr. Brand, affably beginning to ornament his main fact with supplementary details; " he has been sighing ten years, it seems!"

" I always thought he looked as if he had

a history," says Bell, in her south-wind voice;
" if you remember, I said so."

" I do not believe a word of it!" cries
Diana, darting one hasty lightning glance
towards her cousin, and speaking with trembling young voice and poppy-red cheeks;
" as he is the only person of the least consequence in the neighbourhood, they must
always be talking of him : sometimes they
marry him ; sometimes they make him elope
with other people's wives ; sometimes they
break his ribs out hunting ; and never—never
is there the least grain of truth in it !"

" I am sorry to be obliged to contradict a
lady !" rejoins Mr. Brand affably still, though
with a slight streak of offence in his tone at
having the authenticity of his intelligence
impugned ; " but if I tell you that it came
from Mrs. Wolferstan herself, you will perhaps allow that his mother is not unlikely
to be well informed."

" She will be old Mrs. Wolferstan, now,
really," says Bell, simpering, " in contradis-

tinction to young Mrs. Wolferstan. I wonder how she will like that."

"I recollect her now, perfectly!" cries Mrs. Moberley, in a tone of victory, having apparently during the last few moments been raking in the ashes of her memory for Miss Beauchamp; "a dashing-looking girl, with fine falling shoulders! — a shade too stout, perhaps, but that is a criticism that comes ill from me, you will say!" (with a good-humoured laugh).

"And when is it to be?" asks Bell, in her softest stock-dove tone, suited to the tender theme. "Is there any time named? Easter? Whitsun?"

"Easter! Whitsun!" repeats Mr. Brand derisively. "Do you think that a man who has been languishing ten years is likely to defer his bliss much longer? It is to be at once! at once! You may depend on the accuracy of my information!" (with a rather defiant glance towards Diana). "I make a point of never repeating mere *on dits.*"

"There will be plenty of gay doings, no doubt!" cries Mrs. Moberley, a frisky sparkle in her eye, scenting the carnage from afar, like a glad old vulture. "They kept it up pretty well when he came of age; and of course there will be double as much now!—a man's marriage is twice as important an event as his majority, any day."

"The one he can help, the other he cannot!" says Micky, with levity.

"Joan!" cries Bell, in a tone of ecstacy; "Joan, you were right!—you prophesied that something would spring up for us, from a quarter we least expected! I believe you were in the secret!"

"Miss Joan has not given us her opinion yet!" says Mr. Brand, eyeing Miss Dering with that mixture of hurt vanity and loath admiration with which he usually regards her. "We have not heard the sound of your voice yet, Miss Joan! Have you nothing to say?"

At his voice Joan starts a little and slightly

shivers. One of these dream people is speaking to her, and she must answer him. Even at this numb moment some instinct of self-preservation—(in her present half-stunned state it can be scarcely more than an instinct)—prompts her to pull herself together; feebly to lay hold of whatever defensive armour she can find against Micky Brand's pity—against the compassion of the barracks. By a great effort of will she even forces the colour to stay in her cheeks—enough colour, at least, in this kind and shifty firelight, to save her from the imputation of any excessive or livid pallor. She curves her disobedient lips into a stiff set smile.

"You were all talking so fast!" she says, in a low quick voice—(but then her voice is always low, never in highest excitement shrill or clamorous). "I was waiting for an opening. What does one say when one hears that one's acquaintances are going to be married?—that one is very glad? that one hopes it will turn out well? that one wishes they would send over some wedding-cake ?—I am so fond of wedding-cake ! you are too, are not you, Aunt Moberley ?"

" There are worse things !" replies Mrs. Moberley tersely; " but " (shaking her head) " they never send cake now, I am told !— however" (in a more buoyant tone), "perhaps the Colonel may make an exception in favour of you; you and he were always rather friends, and, indeed" (with a little accent of harmless complacence), " I do not think he disliked any of us !"

" No, he did not dislike any of us !" repeats Joan in a mechanical parrot tone.

" I wonder now," continues Mrs. Moberley in a voice of brisk and alert interest, "whether it is in the Helmsley paper this week !—the *Courier* gets hold of anything wonderfully soon. Diana, run and ask whether the *Courier* has come yet."

" May Joan go instead of me ?" asks Diana hastily, and reddening again ; " I—I—I am afraid of the draughts for my cold !"

With a feeling of vague blunt gratitude Joan rises and walks steadily to the door. Once outside it, she reels and staggers against the wall. The sickly gas jet is multiplied to a hundred, which all seem to be dancing and flaring round her. Is she going to faint? What! fall down, and cause them all to come running out and find her swooned, and to guess, not obscurely, the cause. She will die first! She totters to the stairs, and holding tightly to the banisters, slowly climbs to the upper story.

In her own garret she will at least find solitude and darkness. But will she? As she opens the door, a light strikes upon her dismayed eyes; the light of a tallow candle set on the floor beside Sarah, who, in a bear-like and plantigrade attitude, is executing some repairs on the veteran drugget. What malign spirit has prompted her, to-day of all days, to this exercise of unwonted and untimely industry, who shall say? Joan softly recloses the door, with something of the feeling with which—we may suppose—a hard-run fox finds his earth stopped. Whither can she turn? She dare not betake herself to the girls' room; at any moment they may come flying upstairs, and find her face in the dishabille of its utter despair. She descends the stairs again, and when she has reached the foot her eyes fall on the door that leads to the garden. In a moment she has opened it—it is never locked—and now, hatless, cloakless, protectionless, stands in the wintry weather outside.

The night is pitch dark. It clothes her round like a soft close vesture. Dark as it is, she knows so well every inch of the little territory, that now, without any hesitation or faltering, she makes her way between the inky flower-beds—over the dark invisible grass to the sun-dial. At its base she falls down. Her arms encircle its dark pillar. Her delicate flower face is pressed against the cold and obdurate stone. At least, on this January night, they will not think of seeking her here! For some time she lies half unconscious; then, by and by, the raw air, piercing through her gown and chilling her blood, officiously recalls her to life.

"Already — already!" she says, with a moan; "it is too soon! indeed it is too soon! if he had had any humanity, he would have waited a little!—with a whole long life ahead of him—he could afford to wait!"

Another interval. After a while she sits upright, shuddering a little. The nipping wind has brought her back to full consciousness, more quickly than any cordial could have done. A shiver—half of physical cold, half of utter forlornness—shakes her slight body from head to foot. Her woful head falls forward on her knees. This pain is coming to her now in all its sharpness; she has no narcotic to dull it.

"Unstable as water!" she says, with a groan; then, with a most bitter heart-wrung smile, "Why do I blame him? he could not help it! it was his instinct! does one blame any animal for following its instinct? it was his way !—and now this is his way too ! Oh, God ! why do you allow people to have such ways ?" Another longer pause ; then, in a broken voice of utter tenderness : "Oh, my dear, I do not blame you ! it was my own doing ! Great God ! are not all the things that hurt us most our own doing ?"

She is shivering violently, and her teeth chatter with the cold ; this January blast cuts like a knife. She is glad. The discomfort of her body mitigates a little the misery of her soul. She does not know how long she has remained thus, when a noise rouses her ; the sound of the front door opened and again shut ; footsteps crunching the wet gravel of the drive ; the dogs pattering and bow-wowing after Mr. Brand, to see him well off the premises. Probably — nay, certainly, their noses will scent her out here, and discover her. From the inside of the house she hears a voice loudly and gaily calling, " Joan ! Joan ! where are you ? what have you done with the *Courier* ? Joan ! Joan !"

She raises herself to her feet. How black this night is! when she stretches out her hand before her she cannot see it; and yet to-morrow it will be drawn away like a veil from the earth's face; it will be swept away, abolished, blotted out. Oh that she might be abolished, blotted out too—this Joan that is all pain! oh that the night would carry her too away in the sweep of its ebon skirts!

END OF VOL. II.

BILLING AND SONS, PRINTERS, GUILDFORD, SURREY

www.ingramcontent.com/pod-product-compliance
Lightning Source LLC
Chambersburg PA
CBHW021841070726
47496CB00022B/1801